MW00907518

MONSTERS of L.A.

MONSTERS
of L.A.

Lisa
Morton

BAD MOON
BOOKS

ANAHEIM—CALIFORNIA

FIRST EDITION

Monsters of L.A.
© 2011 by Lisa Morton

Cover Photo © 2011 by Lisa Morton

This book is a work of fiction. Names, characters, places and incidents are either a product of the author's imagination or are used fictitiously. Any resemblance to actual events, locales or persons, living or dead, is entirely coincidental.

Interior Design & Typesetting
by César Puch

Copy Editing
by David Marty & Steve Souza

Bad Moon Books Logo Created by Matthew JLD Rice

ISBN-10: 0-9837799-3-7
ISBN-13: 978-0-9837799-3-3

 BAD MOON BOOKS
1854 W. Chateau Ave.
Anaheim, CA 92804
USA

www.badmoonbooks.com

Dedication

This book is dedicated to all the wonderful L.A. area destinations that have vanished over my lifetime and that meant something to me: Aardvark's Odd Ark (Los Angeles), The Ackermansion (Los Feliz), Asahiya Bookstore (Little Tokyo), Beadle's Cafeteria (Pasadena), Berg's Magic Shop (Hollywood), Burbage Theatre (West Los Angeles), Capitol Records Swap Meet (Hollywood), Change of Hobbit (Santa Monica), Dalt's (Toluca Lake), Dangerous Visions (Sherman Oaks), Dave's Laser (Studio City), Garfield Theater (Alhambra), Gorky's (Hollywood), Hallowed Haunting Grounds (Studio City), Happy Land DVDs (Monterey Park), Hinshaw's Department Store (Arcadia), Howard Lowery Animation Gallery (Burbank), Howe's Market (North Hollywood), Lionstar Theatre (Studio City), Old Spaghetti Factory (Hollywood), Papa Bach's (Westwood), Pickwick's Bookstore (Hollywood), Rhino Records (Westwood), Rialto Theater (South Pasadena), Santa's Village (Crestline), and Weby's Bakery (Studio City). I'm thankful for what we've still got in this city, but I sure miss these joints.

Acknowledgments

Let's get the usual suspects out of the way — The Dark Delicacies Writing Group, Roy and Liz and the rest of the Bad Moon bunch, Ricky — and focus on thanking a few of the artists and others who have influenced and inspired my personal take on L.A.

Writers: Dennis Etchison, Steve Erickson, James Ellroy, Charles Bukowski. Filmmaker: David Lynch. Musicians: The Doors. Architects: Paul Williams, Frank Gehry. Artists: Emil Kosa Jr., David Hockney. Children's illustrator: Leo Politi. Nonfiction writer: Horace Bell. Entrepreneurs: Walt Disney, Walter Knott, Henry Huntington. Pompous ass: Griffith J. Griffith.

Extra huge acknowledgment to my favorite wizards of L.A. magic, Tom and Bari Burman.

Table of Contents

MONSTERS
of L.A.

INTRODUCTION

According to the 2010 Census, Los Angeles is the second biggest city in the U.S., home to about 3.8 million people. And 20 monsters.

Of course, L.A. has more than 20 monsters; it probably has tens of thousands, if you take into account all the hustlers, gangbangers, white-collar criminals, street crazies, and other assorted badasses living here. But these 20 are *famous*. These 20 are the rock stars of the monster world. These 20 are Hollywood legends.

The monsters chosen for this collection weren't culled from the pages of literature or mythology or history, because let's face it: L.A.'s an industry town, and the industry is movies. The dreams made here are exported to the entire world, and Tinseltown's fright-mongers are the planet's nightmares.

In these pages you'll find the dark stars you grew up watching: Frankenstein, Dracula, Mr. Hyde, the Phantom, the Hunchback…all the silent ones and the first to find their voices are here, and they're even presented in roughly the order in which they first appeared on a silver screen. The Haunted House of the '30s gives way to the Werewolf of the '40s, the

Creature of the '50s, and so on, all the way up to our favorite modern boogeyman, the Zombie. In some of these stories, you'll find an earthly incarnation of a famous namesake: Frankenstein is a patched-together, homeless vet, the Invisible Woman is so ordinary you'd never see her; but some of these familiar friends—Dracula, the Devil, or those seriously creepy Clowns—will be instantly recognizable. Some of the stories connect with others—what, after all, would The Bride be without her Frankenstein? Some are on the lighter side (really, a Kaiju stomping across Santa Monica can *never* be serious) some prod the tragedy out of horror, but most live snugly in L.A.'s dark side.

And they have two things in common: they all represent an icon of the motion pictures, and they all throw a klieg light on some contemporary part of L.A., the city where I was born, raised, and continue to live.

You probably already know the monsters. After reading this collection, I hope you'll also know a little more about my L.A.

—Lisa
February 11, 2011

MONSTERS
of L.A.

FRANKENSTEIN

FRANKENSTEIN

Frank caught himself on the edge of the liquor store counter and grimaced, swallowing back the pain. It was cold out today, a chill marine breeze blowing in off the Santa Monica bay, the kind of wind that bit through skin and went right for bone. Damn, everything hurt today—even the leg that hadn't been there in forty years.

"You okay, Mr. Frank?" That was the Korean kid behind the counter. Frank tried to remember his name (Ken? Kim?) and finally gave up. He did like how polite the kid always was, though; he was probably the only person left in the world who called Frank "Mister."

"It's way too cold and I'm way too old."

The kid grinned. "That rhymes. Maybe you a rapper."

"Yep. I'm a poet and I know it." Another little stab hit Frank, and he grimaced. "And now I better stow it."

"You need more medicine."

Frank repositioned his cane and turned, trying to grin. "Yeah, sure, but what I can get right now is more gin." He made his way past bottles of tequila and vodka and rum until he found the gin. Yesterday he'd gotten lucky and scored on an entire trash bin full of returnable bottles, so today he had enough for a fifth. In an hour he'd be sprawled on his tattered old blanket under the freeway overpass, feeling good for a precious few hours.

If he were really lucky, he'd never wake up.

But Frank figured his luck had deserted him a long, long time ago. About the time when his 19-year-old self got called up in the draft, plucked out of his small Arizona town and shipped off to 'Nam, where three months in he'd stepped on a mine. One minute he'd been feeling sweat run down his sides as he realized what his foot rested on, and the next he'd been in a hospital in Los Angeles, looking up at a young doctor who was saying something about trying to save what they could, and amputation, and metal implants, and lengthy recovery. His name hadn't been Frank then—it'd been Danny Moss, and he'd once had thick red hair and a dimpled smile that all the girls in high school had loved. But then he'd been blown apart, and he'd ended up with his scalp half burned away and a scar on his jaw, with one leg missing and the other not working too well, with wires in his arms and shrapnel in his spine; and when they'd told him he couldn't stay in the hospital anymore and he'd found himself on the streets of L.A., his new brothers had called him "Frankenstein," and finally just Frank. For a while he'd had a prosthetic leg, but when that had cracked and the V.A. hadn't provided a new one, he'd settled for just letting one pants leg dangle, empty, as he hobbled along on a cane.

He'd tried to readjust, sure. They'd given him vocational training repairing radios, but all the drugs he had to take just to get through a day without screaming made it impossible for him to concentrate. Frank had lost a line of jobs, until he'd found himself on the streets of Santa Monica, panhandling for change, feeling the old wounds hurt more every year, knowing that as his skin was weathered by the mean streets and his teeth fell out, he just grew uglier and uglier. For a year he'd had Lizzie in his life; sweet Lizzie, who'd gotten them a room in a special project to help the homeless, and who'd cleaned herself up from meth addiction and even gotten a job as a waitress. Lizzie, who he'd once proposed to and she'd accepted, but before they could get married she'd said she needed a real place to live and she left, and he'd been on the streets again. That'd been ten years ago. He'd thought about her every day while he'd been alone.

Alone, except for his good friend Gin.

He grabbed a bottle of the cheapest stuff ($7.99 for a fifth, generic label) and negotiated his way back up to the front. The Korean (Jin? Jum?) rang him up, put the bottle in a bag, gave him his change and turned away, already busy with something else.

Frank left, and halfway across the parking lot he decided to fuck the law that said he couldn't drink near a liquor store. He leaned against the low cement block wall surrounding the lot, reached into the bag to unscrew the cap, and took a long pull. The alcohol burned going down, and Frank sputtered a little, but he could already feel the agony of his joints easing, the phantom sensations of his missing leg fading.

He took another gulp and idly watched as a gleaming silver Lexus pulled into the lot. It parked, and the man who got out—tall, distinguished, in his early 70s—glanced uncomfortably at Frank before heading into the store.

Frank stared after the man, paralyzed by the force of a memory knocking against his subconscious.

He knew this man. From somewhere, sometime…this man had been important to him. The association was so strong it felt like a physical sensation, something pulling at him. Frank tried to bring up pictures from the parts of his mind that didn't work well—memory, history, recollection. His hometown? No, that didn't seem right. The war? No—he couldn't imagine this man, who exuded confidence and success, trudging on his hands and knees through jungle muck with the other grunts. The hospital?

"Oh, *fuck*," Frank muttered under his breath, as he recalled the man's face, how it'd looked forty years ago as it'd bent over Frank, telling him that one leg was gone, but they'd been able to save the other...

The doctor. This man was the doctor who'd put him back together. For nine months, this man had checked on him daily, as he'd slowly recovered. Some days he'd been by with other doctors, and he'd smiled and received their admiration as he'd pointed out Frank's various surgeries and scars. "Amazing," they'd said. "Very impressive," as they'd nodded at the young doctor admiringly. Doctor Victor—that'd been his name.

He'd saved Frank's life. And damned him in the process.

Gasping, Frank watched the doctor emerge from the liquor store clutching his own small bag. Frank was willing to bet it didn't hold a cheap eight-dollar bottle of gin.

As the doctor punched the button and his car responded with a chirp, Frank lurched forward, leaving his own purchase on the low block wall. "Hey, Doc—Doctor Victor—"

The man hesitated by his car and turned to eye Frank warily. "Yes?"

Frank stopped a few feet from the man. "Do you remember me, Doc? 'Cause I remember you?"

The doctor peered at Frank, squinting against the afternoon sun. "I'm sorry, I'm retired now..."

"Yeah, it was a long time ago. At the V.A. hospital in West-wood." Frank jabbed downward with the cane. "You took this leg off, did a lot of other shit to me too."

"I treated a lot of patients back then…"

"I was there nine months, you saw me every day…"

Victor took a moment, then Frank saw recognition spark in his eyes. "Moss. Daniel Moss."

"Yeah. Well, I mean, back then…everybody calls me Frank now. Y'know—like Frankenstein."

Victor's eyes roamed over Frank, scrutinizing the work. "I remember."

Frank nodded. "Took the leg off. Blew away part of my head, shot metal fragments into my spine. You always said it was a wonder I wasn't paralyzed." Frank pushed back the sleeve of his threadbare, grime-encrusted camo jacket, and showed off a blackened piece of metal extending from his elbow. "Check this out—metal rod started poking out of my arm about two years ago."

"You should have that looked at."

"Why? They'll just operate again, Doc. I figure I've had more than enough of that for a lifetime. And all from *you*."

Victor looked away nervously and reached for the door handle. "I'm very sorry. If I was still practicing I'd say you could come and see me, but I…"

"You should've just let me die, man."

The doctor froze, staring down at Frank with shock, disgust, and pity. "I couldn't do that, Mr. Moss…"

Frank suddenly realized he was crying, but he didn't try to stop the tears that made clean tracks through the grit on his face. "Yeah, you could have. What was I to you, Doc—like a science project? Something you could maybe brag about to your doctor friends? Was that it?"

"No, of course not—"

"Do you know what it's like, living every day in this body? Jesus Christ, Doc, I'm so goddamn ugly they call me fucking Frankenstein. I hurt all the time, all over; and I don't move so good, and I can't focus on things, and they cut off my benefits a few years back, and that was it for me. I'm like trash you throw away—you watch it blow down the street, and you don't try to go after it, because hey—it's just fuckin' trash, right?!"

Frank knew he was shouting, but he didn't care. Victor looked down at him for a few seconds, then thrust a hand into the pocket of his perfectly tailored slacks and removed his wallet. He pulled two twenties out and handed them to Frank. "Here. I'm really sorry. I thought I could give you another shot at life. I really did."

Frank stared at the money. Part of him wanted to rip the bills from Victor's hand and tear them to pieces, while he told the doctor that he wasn't some goddamn whore who could be paid off to go away, after the doctor had fucked her over...

But his hand almost acted on its own, reaching out to snatch the bills before the doctor reconsidered.

With one last look, Victor said again, "I'm sorry, Daniel."

Frank reached up under his shirt and yanked at a chain he wore there. The doctor stared, mute, as two dog tags fell into his hand.

"They call me Frank now."

Victor clenched a fist around the tags, then climbed into his expensive car and drove away.

Frank watched him go, then looked down at the greenbacks now crumpled in his hand. Forty dollars would buy a lot of gin. He could march into the liquor store right now, surprise the Korean kid by buying another bottle. Maybe he'd splurge and buy a twenty-dollar bottle of really good stuff. He could grab a candy bar, too, or some jerky. Hell, he could even go have a real meal—a burger, fries.

He stood there for a long time—it took Frank a while to parse even small problems—and finally he shoved the money in a pocket and hobbled away from the liquor store. He didn't even think about the gin he'd left on the wall.

No, Frank's mind was completely on something else, on what he would do with his new windfall. Several blocks away was an army surplus store; Frank had bought and sold things there before, and had always liked looking at the merchandise kept under glass at the front.

Yes, he thought forty dollars would buy him a mighty sharp knife.

MONSTERS
of L.A.

DR. JEKYLL
& MR. HYDE

DR. JEKYLL & MR. HYDE

Dr. Jekyll gazed at the syringe and wondered (again) how it would feel to be a man.

"Doctor…?"

Jekyll twitched, then realized the voice came from her assistant, Gabrielle. The pretty young grad student was leaning in the door, pulling on a coat. "If you don't need me anymore tonight…"

"No, it's fine Gabrielle. Thank you."

Gabrielle didn't leave. Instead she edged into the lab, and Jekyll grew anxious, even though Gabrielle knew all about the research.

"It's after 9 p.m. and you look tired."

"I promise I won't stay much longer." Jekyll offered a smile that she hoped would look merely tired, not insincere.

Leaning forward, Gabrielle read over the notes on the glowing computer screen. "It's done, isn't it?"

Jekyll nodded. "Well, there's still the dosage question…"

"You know you'd have patients lining up to help test it."

"I know, but…"

Gabrielle stepped back. "But what? This is the ultimate

answer for gender reassignment. From now on transitioning could be accomplished with only minimal surgery and trauma. You'll make history with this, Doctor Haley Jekyll."

Jekyll stretched, trying to convey fatigue. "That's very kind of you, but we've still got a ways to go. Now, I know you've got something better to do than stay here on a Friday night."

Gabrielle grimaced. "Not really. That idiot Joe is coming over tonight, but I'm getting pretty tired of him."

"Oh. Sorry to hear that."

"I'm not."

Gabrielle hesitated, then turned to leave. Jekyll waited until the door was closed and she heard Gabrielle's footsteps exiting the building.

She took off her lab coat.

Dr. Jekyll knew Gabrielle was right—she could have asked one of her patients; any of them would probably have jumped at the chance—but she couldn't approach them without considerable safeguards and standards in place, nor could she rely completely on their assessment of the drug's success. No, the typical clinical trials, with double-blind procedures, could follow later. First, she needed a single test on the perfect subject. Someone who could objectively assess the drug's effects, who had always been curious about the opposite sex, who had deliberately placed herself outside the battle of the sexes so she could observe from a cool distance.

She rolled up her sleeve.

She'd already prepared a letter detailing what she was about to do, in case it proved unsuccessful, even deadly. She'd waited until Friday night—tonight—to be sure her offices at UCLA would be deserted. Gabrielle had just left, and the other doctors were long gone. Now was the time.

Dr. Jekyll turned on a webcam and spoke into it briefly. "Test #1 with XG14, at a dosage of point-five m-l. Date is October 2nd, time is 9:24 p.m." She rubbed her arm with a sterile swab, laid the needle flat against the vein, took a deep breath—and injected herself.

The effect was instantaneous.

The syringe fell to the floor, forgotten, as Dr. Jekyll was seized by an electrifying rush. She gasped as she felt the changes in her body: her blood was on fire, her skin was pierced by millions of tiny new follicles, her muscles writhed as they grew and flexed. When she felt the cloth of her silk blouse constrict around her, she tore at it blindly; and it came away like tissue paper in her strong grasp. Her skirt rippled with the changes in her body. Her throat burned as physiology rearranged, lengthened, deepened.

When she could think again, she realized she was on the floor, staring down at a lightly furred hand with large, powerful knuckles and blunt nails. Her gazed traveled up the arm, tracing the outline of sinews she'd never seen, the swell of muscles she hadn't owned a moment ago. She felt her face and laughed as she found stubble; the sound of her voice was deep, and she felt it resonate in her throat.

The power was all consuming. Dr. Jekyll forgot objectivity and reportage in a sudden urge to run, to feel his heart pumping and muscles thrumming.

He leapt from the floor and started for the door, then caught sight of the shreds of clothing and stopped. He remembered that Jekyll kept workout sweats in the closet, and he changed quickly. Garbed in baggy gray, he left the constricting offices behind.

Outside, the night air was cool and exhilarating, and Dr.

Jekyll ran, for the sheer joy of his new physicality. His stride was long and smooth, his lungs working efficiently; and he gloried in his energy. In a few minutes, as he ran the up-and-down, curving road that encircled the dark campus, he began to sweat; and the moisture on his heated skin felt like a glass of ice water offered by a lover on a summer day.

At some point, he finally paused and found himself at the far northwest end of the campus, near the student dormitories. He realized he still wore his watch (a silly feminine thing with flexible gold band and small face) and was startled to see it was after midnight. A slight fog had slithered east from the coast and covered Westwood, rendering the tall dorm buildings as half-seen glowing monoliths.

Jekyll heard a light male laugh and stepped off the walkway into the safe shadows, curious.

A boy was approaching; Jekyll heard him first, the fog rendering vision obsolete and because the boy's conversation was one-sided, Jekyll knew he must be talking on his cell. Finally the boy's dim form materialized, approaching as he continued to jabber about a concert he'd been to and an instructor he disliked. His voice told Jekyll he probably wasn't even twenty yet, and the first sight of him confirmed the guess. No more then 19, with shaggy blond hair, a narrow, handsome face, slim build.

The lust that surged through Jekyll was as startling and unexpected as the muscular power had been earlier. Jekyll's entire being was suddenly centered in his crotch, and he felt his hips pulled forward as if by some outside force.

The female Dr. Jekyll had been alone for almost two years. Her fiancé had called off their marriage when he'd realized that her work mattered far more than he ever would, and when confronted she hadn't denied that. She'd buried herself in her patients during the day and her research at night; she returned home exhausted, with weekends reserved only for simple domestic chores. She knew she didn't have the easy path that most of her male colleagues, with their connections and networks, had, so she worked harder. She would have admitted that the boy was attractive—in fact, she might even have secretly noticed him once or twice around school—but she would never have acted on the attraction.

Now, however…

Testosterone raced through an adult body that had never experienced it before, and Jekyll was almost subsumed. Primitive instincts—blood and sex, power and lust—coursed in altered veins. There was no time to objectively examine what he was experiencing; all of Jekyll's concentration was funneled to control.

Jekyll must have made a sound (a howl? Groans of agonized restraint?) because the boy paused, glanced back, and abruptly finished his call. He peered through the fog for a moment, then turned and started walking fast, almost a run, for the sanctuary of the dorms.

Jekyll lost the battle for possession; the boy couldn't be allowed to reach safety or call for help—help that might reveal Jekyll and the experiment. He leapt after the boy and overtook him quickly, throwing an arm around the young neck and pulling the struggling young man into the brush away from the path. The boy kicked and squirmed and tried to shout, but Jekyll's other arm went to his mouth, muffling his cries. As his oxygen supply was cut off, fight slowly left the boy, and finally his struggles faded.

Jekyll dropped the boy's body to the ground and straddled him, frantically undoing belt and zipper. He tugged the boy's jeans and boxers down, felt his own hips buck in excitement—and suddenly realized he wasn't entirely sure what to do. He yanked the sweat pants down, reached for his penis—

—and realized with shock that he didn't really have one. He possessed neither the female Jekyll's organs, nor those that a born male would have had; his penis, forced from Jekyll's body by the drug and lacking surgical enhancement, was little more than a short, hardened nub.

With a cry of furious disappointment, Jekyll pulled the boy's limp body to him, burying himself in the naked torso. He snarled and thrust, and when he felt something warm and wet beneath him it finally brought him to climax. Shuddering, he came in waves of delirious relief until he was spent. Then he rose, pulled the sweat pants up, and staggered into the fog, riding aftershocks of post-coital satisfaction, system reeling from both the synthetic drug and the natural intoxicant.

A few minutes later he began to tire, and rationality returned. He knew the drug's effects were ebbing; his strength was failing, his energy depleted. He turned his faltering steps toward Jekyll's office and had just barely enough stamina left to lock the door behind him before he passed out.

It was Saturday afternoon when Jekyll awoke. She rose slowly, groggy and bleary-eyed, until she saw the blood that covered her. She remembered the boy from the night before and knew exactly what she'd done.

The boy was dead. Now Jekyll wore his blood.

She started to be sick, but forced it down. She had to think. Had she left a trail of blood leading straight to her office? Then she heard something outside, and relief washed over her.

It was raining. Last night's fog had become a storm, and she heard pounding water lash the roof overhead. That was why it was late afternoon and she wasn't in jail already: the rain had washed away the trail.

She staggered to the office bathroom and washed the dried blood from her arms and hands. She was disgusted to see splatters on her face and neck, and she scrubbed at them frantically, then made sure the sink was spotless. She'd have to return home for a change of clothes, but…

She knew she should turn herself in. Now, with her clothes stained by the boy's life.

But…the drug hadn't exactly failed. It was just a matter of adjusting the dosage. It could still help her patients, and all of the others who had been born into the wrong body. If she turned herself in now, her triumph would never see the light of day. She couldn't do it, not when she was so close. She'd wait and surrender after, when she knew her work would survive and benefit others. Surely that was the right, the most moral, course of action.

Was she even sure the boy was dead?

She headed to her computer and brought up the *L.A. Times* website. A quick scan of local stories revealed what she dreaded: A young man had been found brutally murdered on the UCLA campus, near the dormitory buildings. The body of Calvin Baxter Arendt, 19, had been discovered early Saturday morning by a jogger; police were saying only that the gruesome slaying involved disembowelment. At this time there was no known motive and no suspects.

Jekyll fell back in her chair, too horrified to move. She renewed her determination to turn herself in. Then she saw the webcam she'd turned on last night. It was shut off now, but had recorded several hours. She brought up the video file, opened it, and watched.

There she was last night, with the needle hovering above the flesh of her elbow. There she was, bent double in shock as she felt her body change. And there *he* was, rising up, his face subtly re-shaped, stubbled growth on jawline and cheek, brows thickened, throat displaying a fresh new lump. He cleared his throat and the effect was startling—a gruff, deep, very masculine sound.

And his eyes—*her* eyes—were wild. They glittered with feral cunning and mad energy. Dr. Jekyll saw him tear at his constricting female clothing before he skittered out of frame and was lost to the recording.

But she'd seen enough.

She immediately deleted the video file, double-checked the recycle bin to make sure it was completely gone, then gathered all the evidence from last night—clothing, stained paper towels—and loaded them into a plastic bag. She threw on a white coat, hiked the short distance to the nearest lab, and deposited the bag in a hazardous waste disposal bin.

Then Jekyll drove home, took an hour-long shower, and fell into bed, where she tried not to think about Calvin Baxter Arendt.

Two weeks later, she was ready to try again.

Jekyll had adjusted figures and formulae, been over and over the numbers and the measurements; she'd gotten little sleep, and Gabrielle had frequently begged her to slow down.

Once again she chose a Friday evening, but this time she made a few changes. She had men's clothing on hand. And she had a second syringe nearby, full of heavy sedative. She believed she could monitor herself (himself) and use the syringe if the drug again produced unexpected results.

But she knew it wouldn't.

She locked the lab door and remembered to undress. She again turned on the videocam, made a few preliminary notes, and readied the injection.

A smooth shot, into the left arm…

There was no excruciating pain this time, no sense of her body tearing itself apart and rebuilding. It took longer—three full hours—although the sensations were strange, they felt right.

When Jekyll looked into the mirror at last, he once again saw his sturdy, lightly bearded face, but this time without the wildness in the eyes. He felt calm and centered.

Jekyll dressed himself quickly, made notes, and then decided to test his body with a short walk. He realized he was hungry and remembered that there were several late-night eateries in the village. Remembering that Jekyll had left her purse in her office, he locked the lab behind him, walked the short distance to the office, and entered.

He retrieved money from the wallet, then had to remind himself not to carry the purse. He was just leaving the office when a figure appeared in the doorway.

"Oh," uttered a surprised feminine voice, "I didn't realize anyone was here…"

It was Gabrielle.

Jekyll stood stunned for a second, as if he were a small child caught stealing a candy bar; but when he realized Gabrielle didn't recognize him, he forced himself to relax slightly.

"Sorry, I was just leaving. I was supposed to meet my cousin Haley here, but she hasn't showed."

Gabrielle did look at him carefully now and smiled slightly. Jekyll had never realized quite how pretty she was, with a grin that tilted up slightly on one side and brown eyes flecked with sienna.

"Cousin, huh?" Gabrielle stepped forward. "Well, I can certainly see the resemblance. I'm her assistant, Gabrielle Utterson."

Jekyll thrust a hand forward and enjoyed the feeling of her soft fingers in his steady, firm grip. "Hi, Gabrielle. She's told me about you."

"She has?"

"Oh, yes." Jekyll suddenly realized he was expected to supply a name; he thought about his real cousin, Edward, and he thought about his tough new skin. "I'm Edward Hyde. But please call me Eddie."

"Hi. So Haley was supposed to meet you here and didn't show? That's not like her."

"She did warn me that she might be late getting back from some errand. How about you? Do you normally visit the office after midnight?"

"No, but…well, I just dumped this guy I've kind of been seeing, and I needed something to take my mind off the idiot, so I thought I'd just come here and work…"

"You sound like the perfect assistant."Jekyll looked down again at Gabrielle's long, silky blond hair and narrow chin, and was struck with inspiration. "I was about to go grab a bite on my own. Listen, if you're not doing anything…?"

Gabrielle considered briefly, then turned that enticing half-smile on Jekyll again. "You know what? I'd love to. Let's go."

Jekyll hesitated only long enough to assure himself that the warmth coursing through him was happiness.

They ate at a noisy student hangout just off-campus, shouting to be heard over music and voices. When they finished, they gratefully left the din behind and strolled the streets of Westwood, still crowded at 2 a.m., but at least not deafening. They talked of school and work and dreams, and Jekyll was surprised and pleased by the admiration Gabrielle expressed for her mentor.

As a distant bell struck a new hour, Gabrielle made a sudden decision, turned to Jekyll and said, "Do you want to come back to my place? We could just…y'know, hang and watch an old movie or something."

Jekyll knew he should say no. He should return to the lab and examine himself, test vitals, record findings. He knew the low dosage he'd administered this time wasn't intended to last long; he could suddenly find himself in an embarrassing position with Gabrielle, whose trust was vital to the success of his work.

But, intrigued by both Gabrielle and the workings of his new body, he said yes.

Jekyll had seen Gabrielle's apartment, of course, and had to remind himself to seem curious about it. He inquired about her choice of art (a Van Gogh print) and her bookshelves (textbooks and mystery novels); he politely declined her offer of a nightcap (he couldn't risk mixing alcohol and the drug) but had no objection when she indulged.

"That's funny," she said, peering at him, "Haley doesn't drink either."

And when she kissed him, he responded with surprising passion.

They pulled apart, and Gabrielle—more than a little drunk—laughed slightly. "Well, that was a surprise."

Jekyll smiled and drew her hair through his fingers, luxuriating in the sensation. "Why?"

"I didn't think you liked sex much."

A stab of anxiety lanced through Jekyll, but he reminded himself that Gabrielle was drunk, that she probably hadn't realized what she was saying. He kissed her, letting his tongue linger on her lips, then he breathed into her ear, "Now why would you say that?"

She pulled back and looked at him carefully. "I know who you are... *Haley.*"

Jekyll froze.

Gabrielle laughed slightly. "I figured it out at dinner. You ordered what you always order. You ate it the way you always eat it. And I knew you'd try the drug on yourself first."

"I..." Jekyll cleared a throat suddenly too dry to produce speech. "But you...asked me here, you kissed me..."

"I wanted to know. Didn't you?"

Jekyll relaxed. "I still do."

Their tongues found each other in the next kiss, breath quickened, desire flooded Jekyll.

And with desire came bloodlust.

He gasped and pulled back from Gabrielle's grip. She opened her eyes and looked at him, perplexed. "What's wrong?"

"I...nothing."

Jekyll awoke in her lab the following day. She hurt from apparently having slept on the cold tile floor, and her male clothes hung loosely about her slender frame. Her head throbbed; her hands were sticky.

Sticky?

From the blood.

She stared in shock, searched her memory. Blood? Whose blood? From where from when, how?

The last thing she remembered was kissing Gabrielle. Her assistant. Who'd known.

Jekyll ran to the mirror and saw she was covered in dried blood—on her arms, splattered on her neck, even a clot in her hair. She rubbed frantically at one stain on her forehead, but still no recollection came.

She rushed to the lab phone and dialed Gabrielle's cell number from heart. After a few rings it was answered—by a deep, older male voice.

"Oh, sorry—I'm trying to reach Gabrielle Utterson…"

"Who is this?"

Jekyll knew: The man answering Gabrielle's phone was a homicide detective, and she was dead. Murdered, last night.

By Eddie Hyde.

She blurted out something about being Gabrielle's boss and having a work question, and the man confirmed all of her suspicions. Jekyll tried to sound appropriately shocked. It wasn't hard.

She hung up the phone and fell back, drained, considering.

There was no choice this time—she had to turn herself in. Maybe she could get a plea bargain and wouldn't be looking at life imprisonment. But no, she'd slain twice now; surely there would be no mercy accorded to her. To *him*.

But did she deserve such punishment? After all, it hadn't strictly been her committing these crimes; it'd been a man. A jury might not understand that, but she did. And the drug could still be useful; if she surrendered to a life in prison, was she depriving those still struggling with gender transformation of a better, easier life?

She tried to go over her experiences clinically. Last night's test had been completely successful in every regard until… what? What had changed?

Sexual arousal. Of course. Kissing Gabrielle had ignited Hyde's own response; the resulting chemical changes in Hyde's body had created a blackout and violent impulses. Was it because she'd used the wrong dosage the first time?

That made sense. It was just a matter of adjusting the dosage down from the beginning. Which meant the drug was still viable.

And she couldn't give herself up.

The decision was made, then. She'd continue her research, remain hidden. It should be possible—the police would be looking for a man, and as long as she didn't test the drug on herself again, that man didn't exist.

Eddie Hyde was dead. There would be only Haley Jekyll from now on.

The police did come to the office on Monday.

They told Jekyll that witnesses in the restaurant had seen Gabrielle with a slightly built man, mid-to-late-thirties, brown hair, light beard. Because they thought the same man had raped and murdered Calvin Arendt, they thought it might be a bisexual or transitioning individual, possibly a patient who had even known Gabrielle. Jekyll told them none of her patients fit that profile. They asked for access to her files. She told them she'd have to check with the school's legal counsel.

Jekyll didn't sleep that night, or the next few nights afterward. She was tormented by images of Gabrielle, with her silken hair, perfect skin, and cocked smile. Alone in her bed, late at night, she thought of Gabrielle and felt her own body stir; and the feeling created confusion and frustration. She'd never been attracted to women, so she thought this was some remnant of Hyde still attached to her psyche like a malignant barnacle. Or had she simply never acknowledged her own sexuality, and Hyde had made it easy for her? The possibilities chased each other through her head like a circle of hounds nipping at each others' paws.

And sometimes, when she thought of Gabrielle's face and body…she felt Hyde begin to rise within her, and she forced him down.

Although philosophy had never been Jekyll's strong point—she preferred facts to abstractions—she found her mind returning to notions of man's dual nature. It was nothing as naïvely simple as good and evil, she decided, but was much more a question of the duality of man *and* woman: a complex dance of organ and hormone, aggression and nurture, power and compromise. It would be easy, so easy, to give herself over to Hyde and let his masculine strength envelop her, allow his passions to consume the weak, questioning Haley Jekyll…

But it would be the end of them both.

So she tried to keep Hyde hidden, and to continue with Haley Jekyll's rational, loveless existence.

The police returned a week later.

41

They came into Jekyll's office as she sat before the computer, staring in disbelief at the results from the latest round of tests she'd run on herself. The blood work had to be in error. The lab had made a mistake.

But those thoughts vanished as the police presented Jekyll with their news: They had fingerprints and DNA from Gabrielle's apartment. They'd found semen on her corpse.

Jekyll sat speechless for a few seconds; she hadn't considered that the drug would be so effective that Hyde's body would be capable of producing semen after only two shots.

"Dr. Jekyll?" one of the detectives prodded, when she continued to stare in mute disbelief.

She rallied herself and tried to answer their questions. They asked again about her patients. They asked about other doctors. They even asked about relatives.

They asked about her research.

She tried to sound casual as she fed them words and facts they wouldn't understand, and she didn't stop until she saw their eyes glaze over. Then she smiled, added, "That kind of thing" as a joke, and knew she'd won.

She thought they wouldn't be back this time.

They were turning to go when one of the men stopped, reached into a pocket, and produced a small envelope. "Oh, Doctor, there's one more thing I think you should see…"

He held out a stack of color photographs. Jekyll took them, growing dread inside her, already knowing what they were.

The top photos showed the body of Calvin Arendt as it had been found in the undergrowth; beneath those were vivid shots of Gabrielle dead in her bed. Both corpses were pale, bloodied, glassy eyed; the boy was partially disemboweled, the girl's neck marked by heavy blue strangulation marks.

And they were both naked.

Jekyll looked at the photos and felt Hyde wriggle within her.

No.

The images of splattered genitals—the boy's penis, flaccid in death; the girl's vagina, legs still spread—excited Hyde. He battered against Jekyll's resistance, and she began to weaken. She dropped the photos and clutched the edge of her desk.

"I'm sorry, Doctor, I know they're not very pretty…" one of the detectives said.

Jekyll tried to look away, but the photos were there, on the desk just below her; and they'd fallen across the desk so she could see them all at once—

Blood sex power Hyde's seed and open waiting flesh and

Jekyll groaned—and heard Hyde's deeper, rougher tones.

"What the fuck—?" one of the detectives muttered, as he backed away.

The change was happening; Jekyll couldn't stop it. She gave up trying. Hyde would have her, and they would have Hyde.

One of the detectives pulled a gun; the other leapt forward with handcuffs.

As they restrained Hyde, he didn't struggle; he knew they would kill him if he did, and he didn't want to die. Especially not after what Jekyll had seen in the test results, just before the police had come. That knowledge gave Hyde an inward glow of pride and would carry him through the dark days to come.

He was going to be a father.

MONSTERS
of L.A.

THE
PHANTOM

THE PHANTOM

Erica pushes the fat rodent away with the splitting toe of her ancient sneaker. It's time to forage again.

She's still riding the last shot of meth, so she's feeling all right. She pulls the stained cardboard away from the hole in the wall she uses as a door, and the sudden wash of light sends things scampering back into the darkness. But not Erica.

She's still cautious though, so she pulls on her hoodie (even though she's sweating) and arranges the folds around her face. After five years of riding the White Pony, her face—once proclaimed (by *Rolling Stone*, no less) for its "angular beauty"—has sunken and scabbed over, and she doesn't like it when strangers look at her. Especially if she thinks they might recognize her… although it's probably even worse when they don't.

Other tweakers are sleeping, zoned out, or dead around the large building, so she tries to move silently. It's a big place, Loco's is, and Erica—in those moments between the drug's high and low, when Erica's neurons still fire in the right sequence, like now—remembers it as it once was, before meth claimed her and urban decay took Loco's. It'd been one of the great old clubs on the Strip; during the '40s it had hosted big bands and elegant couples, and history claimed that The Doors had once played here in '65. It'd closed for a while in the '70s and '80s, sitting sad and forlorn on Sunset Boulevard, until new owners had tried to reopen it in '95. But they'd never had the money to do it right, and it had closed again in '03.

Erica Cloud had been one of the last acts to play there.

She looks at the stage as it is now—rotting boards, walls peeling or caving in, prone bodies spaced before it like sleeping fans waiting for the show to start—and the sadness almost overwhelms. Not sadness for herself—no, she's never allowed herself that indulgence—but melancholy for this place, Loco's, a part of Los Angeles now left to molder while warring groups battle over whether to claim it as a historical monument, or tear it down and make room for progress. Erica knows that a win for either side (and she's guessing it will be progress, since progress almost always wins) will be a loss for her. She'll have to move on, then.

Cleaning herself up probably isn't an option, not at this point. Not this far gone. And why? So she can be eaten again by the other drug, the one called "fame?" She'd been abused enough by those pushers—the executives who'd praised her and then fired her, the managers who'd praised themselves and then stolen from her, the musicians, producers, and hangers-on who'd loved her and then forgotten her.

So much easier this way.

She's not hungry—she hasn't been hungry in years, despite her thin frame—but she'll need money for dunk soon—so she pushes out into the smoggy Los Angeles day.

Erica's not especially surprised to find that it's already late afternoon, although she curses herself briefly for losing the best scavenging time; others will have beaten her to the best dump-

The Phantom

ster-diving. She doesn't like having to earn money that way, but it's all she's got…now that the music's gone.

A few memories flicker through Erica's head: a guitar in her hands and her fingers find the notes seemingly on their own, the way the crowd won't stop applauding after that first live gig with the band, giggling when she realizes her album has been bootlegged onto a BitTorrent, the plans for the European tour.

The memories end with Mark—beautiful Mark, who'd backed her up on stage and off, who'd played lead guitar and her equally well, whose body had seemingly been able to tolerate anything—suggesting to her one night, five weeks into a string of concerts, when she'd been so exhausted she didn't know how she'd even climb the steps to the stage, that she needed a little pick-me-up. She'd been too tired to argue, and it'd been great at first. But then she'd needed more and more, and focusing on the music had gotten harder and harder, and after the debut CD flopped, their label had dropped them, and at some point—yesterday or five years ago, it made no difference to Erica—she'd crawled into the beautiful derelict on the Sunset Strip and made it her home.

She walks down Sunset, her body at war with itself; the drug is speeding her up, but years of it have made her clumsy, so her walk is a strange, rapid shuffle. She's got some empty plastic bags clutched in one hand, and she hopes to score a few recyclables out of the trash bins from the swanky apartments just to the north of the boulevard. If she can get in and out before getting caught, she can usually find a few dollars worth of glass, plastic, and metal; and that's all she needs.

Erica is about to turn off Sunset when a sound catches her ears—a plaintive tune sung by a high female voice, accompa-

49

nied by a few simple guitar chords. Something about the song *freezes* her, and she stands, ears straining to pick out the notes and words. After a few seconds, she turns and follows the lovely noise like a bloodhound scenting a trail.

There, on the Boulevard, is a girl busking for change. She's young, can't be more than twenty, and pretty, with long red hair and high cheekbones.

Erica remembers herself at 19, coming to L.A. for the first time with no more than a guitar, some songs, and her old car. She'd been pretty then, too, and had made money off singing, although she'd been better than this girl. She'd never had to work street corners; she'd found success quickly in the clubs and the studios. They'd all wanted her. For a while, anyway.

There's an open guitar case at the girl's feet, and it's already filling with change and bills. Erica stops a few feet away from the girl, watching. The girl obviously tries to avoid looking at the homeless woman in front of her, but then the song finishes and she has no choice.

"How are you today?" she says, trying not to sound uncomfortable and failing.

"That song…" Erica can't finish the sentence.

"Oh, it's one of my favorites. It's called—"

Erica finishes for her. "'Red Dreams'."

The girl nods and smiles. "Yeah. You like Erica Cloud?"

Erica chooses to ignore the question. "How do you know that song?"

"Are you kidding? Everybody knows that album."

"But…it flopped…"

Cocking her head, intrigued now, the girl answers, "Yeah, I think it did at first. And it's the only one she ever made. Hey, are you okay?"

Erica hasn't realized she's crying. She shakes her head and turns away, hoping the girl hasn't looked at her too closely. "Sorry. I'll…go."

She wipes her eyes and tries to leave, but suddenly the girl is in front of her, blocking her way. "Wait…take this." The girl extends the bills from the case.

Erica eyes them suspiciously. "Why?"

"Because…I think they're really yours, aren't they?"

After a moment, Erica nods, takes the bills, and walks away. This time the girl lets her go.

Erica shoves the bills into a pocket and remembers the last time she was paid for her songs, how good it felt. It was a better high than anything she's had in years. She suddenly wishes she had a guitar again, and a steady hand, and a nice place to sit while she drinks coffee and writes new songs.

Everybody knows that album…

Her feet start to retrace the path back to Loco's, but her mind forces them away. She goes back to find the girl packing up her guitar, about to leave. The girl looks at her with curiosity, but with something else, too...

"You missed one chord in the second verse. It goes like this—" and Erica hums it perfectly, making strumming motions with her hand.

The girl watches, smiling. "Thanks."

Erica pushes back the hood and lets the girl look at her. The girl's expression falters only for a second—Erica sees the quick glint of horror and pity—then she settles back into awe.

Erica walks on. There's nothing she needs back at Loco's, although she still hopes they save it. She's not sure where she's going, but at this point—somewhere is better than nowhere.

That'd make a great song title, Erica thinks; and she smiles.

MONSTERS
of L.A.

THE
HUNCHBACK

THE HUNCHBACK

Quasimodo is crowned at the Festival of Fools and sings *about being the best man in France.*

"Jordan Moore?"

Jordi's head jerked up, away from the notebook he'd been writing in. Mr. Vint stood at the front of the classroom, his erratic gray eyebrows raised in irritation.

"Uhhh…"

Students snickered at Jordi's confusion. A few desks behind and to his right, he heard Brent Dade whisper something.

"Can you tell me the answer to the problem?"

The teacher gestured at an equation on the blackboard. Jordi peered at it, but the numbers refused to arrange themselves into anything meaningful. He decided that a random guess was better than nothing; maybe he'd get lucky.

"Forty-two?"

The giggles redoubled. Jordi thought he heard Brent mutter, "Fag." He felt his face flush with heat.

Vint sighed. "Mr. Moore, unfortunately not every class can be theater. This is algebra. It would be nice if you could remember a few of your lines here, too."

"Okay, Mr. Vint."

The teacher shot Jordi a final sharp look, then turned to the rest of the class. "Anyone else?"

Jordi tried to return his attention to his math textbook, and he suddenly felt a small sting on the back of his neck. A rubber band fell to the floor, and he turned to see Brent Dade sniggering as he held up a crude drawing of a boy—presumably Jordi—kneeling before Mr. Vint performing oral sex. On either side of Brent, his constant companions Maxx Harrison and Pedro Avila tried to restrain laughter.

Jordi caught their gazes, and then slowly, lasciviously, rolled his tongue across his lips.

The three boys glowered.

Jordi turned back, satisfied. Even if it meant he'd get his ass pounded later, he'd co-opted their attempt to insult him; and he took his small victories where he could.

"Let me help you with the math."

Jordi looked at Alison and laughed. "Girl, you're even worse at that shit than I am."

"I am not!"

They smiled at each other, worked their way through lunch; they never ate in the cafeteria, with all the others, but sat out in the courtyard, which they could do all year round thanks to the San Gabriel valley weather.

Jordi opened his notebook and pushed it across the scarred plastic table to Alison. "I really like this idea of a musical version of *Hunchback of Notre Dame*. I started writing the first song today. Check it out."

Alison scanned the page, speaking a few of the lines:

Look at this face,
It's ugly, so true.
My body is bent,
Not what God surely meant.
But still I am better than you…

She stopped reading and looked up at Jordi. "Is this why you got in trouble during math?"

Jordi nodded. "What do you think?"

"It's great. You should keep going. Maybe we can get Mrs. Lund to really consider staging this for the final project."

"That'd be cool."

Alison glanced past Jordi and frowned. "Uh-oh…Brent Dade is giving you the evil eye."

Jordi didn't even turn. "It'd be so much easier if he'd just admit that he wants to kiss me."

"Jordi, I don't think you should joke about him. Did you know his dad did time for armed robbery? They're all nuts and bullies. Stay away from him."

"Okay. I promise not to ask him to play Esmeralda in *Hunchback*. He can't sing anyway."

That night, Jordi tried to finish his math homework—he couldn't afford to flunk this class, not if he wanted to graduate next year and flee to college where he could major in Theater Arts—but his thoughts kept circling back to his musical. He imagined Quasimodo finishing his ironic song at the Festival of

Fools, only to return to the cathedral and be scolded by Frollo, the cruel Archdeacon and Quasimodo's excuse for a father.

For inspiration, Jordi put on his headphones and opened an album on his phone — Erica Cloud, again — and let himself flow into the lush melody and evocative lyrics. His pencil began to move almost of its own accord, Frollo's song etching itself on a sheet of lined notebook paper. There, in metric rhyme, was his contempt for humanity and his specific loathing of himself, which he directed at Quasimodo.

You're a fool indeed, to believe that they
Can ever do more than fear you and pray —

Jordi heard something over the music — voices, raised in argument. He lowered the headphones and listened for a second.

"—did you see how he was dressed today? For fuck's sake—"

That was his father. There was a soft response he couldn't make out — Mother. As usual, she defended her son — and provoked another shout.

"'Being himself?' Christ, Jen, the fucking kid looks like a West Hollywood drag queen half the time…"

Jordi put the headphones back on, although he knew it wouldn't help much. The argument would end in a few minutes when his father went back to his beer and his videogame, and Mom came into his bedroom to tell him everything was okay.

And all the time he'd sit on his bed and wish they'd all just leave him alone so he could write.

"Hey, faggot—"

As he strode across the school parking lot, Jordi ignored Brent's voice behind him—until he felt a small missile strike his head.

"I'm talking to you, queer."

Jordi spun and locked eyes with Brent, who stood twenty feet away with his entourage. "The name's Jordi."

Brent nodded at something silver on the ground—the thing he'd thrown at Jordi. "Pick that up…*faggot*."

"Why? So you can see my ass when I bend over?" Jordi squirmed provocatively.

Pedro Avila stepped forward, and Jordi felt a small rush of fear; he'd always been more afraid of the quiet, hulking boy with the heavy brow, than slight, pale Brent Dade. "Pick it up."

Jordi considered trying to outrun them, but the parking lot was enclosed by a chain link fence, and they were all faster than he was. There were a lot of other kids around at this hour, but Jordi knew none of them would help. Seeing no alternative, he bent and retrieved the small object.

It was a tube of lipstick. Jordi eyed it critically, then said, "'Desert Sunset.' Nice, but not my color."

Brent took a step forward. "Put it on."

"Isn't your momma gonna whup you when she finds out this is missing? Or did you get it out of Daddy's side of the medicine cabinet?"

Brent's smile broke, and he strode angrily up to Jordi. "I said, put it on, freak."

Jordi raised his hand in the air and held the tube aloft. "I really think it'd look better on you." He dropped the tube deliberately on Brent's foot.

Brent charged.

Jordi hit the pavement hard, enough to knock the air out and leave him dazed; so he was only dimly aware that Brent was sitting atop him while Maxx and Pedro held his arms down. He felt something smearing his face and knew it was the lipstick. He tried to turn away, but his head was slapped back into position hard.

"C'mon, you little freak, you should love this, right? Tell me you love it and maybe I'll stop. Huh? C'mon, let's hear how much you love it—"

Jordi tried to say something, but his tongue felt thick, and he couldn't seem to use it.

He abruptly felt the pressure on his left arm ease, and he heard Maxx say something about teachers coming. Pedro also rose, but Brent wasn't quite finished—he jammed the lipstick between Jordi's crimsoned lips and hissed, "That's a little present for you, because I know how much you like to suck on things."

Then they were gone.

Jordi knew there were other kids watching, but his strength was gone, and no one offered to help him up; no teachers arrived, no hand was offered.

Until he heard a voice, "Jordi? Jordi, oh my God—"

Alison.

She pushed past the gawking kids around Jordi and knelt by him, her hands fluttering over him like panicked birds. "Are you okay? What happened? Can you hear me—?"

Jordi groaned and tried to sit up, but he couldn't do it—until he felt Alison's hand on his back. "I think I'm okay. Just give me a minute."

"Is that blood…?"

Jordi wiped a hand across his face and held his red-stained fingers out to her. "Lipstick. Courtesy of my new makeup man

Brent."

Alison glanced back, her features creased in anger. "Brent. We're going to the principal this time…"

"No, Ally. Please, don't." Jordi struggled to his feet, helped by Alison. "I can handle Brent."

Alison started to say something, then turned instead and yelled at two girls who stood nearby, not moving. "And thanks a lot for helping. Enjoy the show?"

The girls turned away wordlessly.

"Fuck them," she snarled.

"Sorry — not my type," Jordi answered, before turning to limp to the nearest bathroom.

The Hunchback looks up from the stocks as Esmeralda sings to him.

Jordi tried to work on the song, but the lyrics were slow in coming, partly because he hurt all over — he'd sustained more bruises from Brent's attack than he'd realized. But the real block was that he wanted Esmeralda to sing about the importance of compassion, and he didn't feel very compassionate tonight.

He tried to imagine Alison's voice, clear and sweet, and the words came. She'd never sung in front of an audience before, but she'd sung to Jordi for his birthday, and she was good. If Mrs. Lund agreed to produce Jordi's *Hunchback*, he was going to insist on Alison for Esmeralda.

And he, of course, would be Quasimodo.

> *I'll quench your thirst*
> *I can do this first*

But I can't give you
The life that you crave
The heart that would save
Your world and make it all true.

The next day, Jordi decided to show Mrs. Lund what he'd done so far on *Hunchback*.

The drama class was prepping a production of *Spoon River Anthology*. Jordi, who was running lights and sound, waited until a break in the scene being rehearsed and approached Mrs. Lund with his small sheaf of papers. She eyed the first few pages, smiled at him, and told him she'd read it tonight.

Jordi found Alison waiting for him after class. "Jordi, I —"

He cut her off, excited. "Mrs. Lund's going to read what I've done on *Hunchback* so far. I think she'll go for it, Ally. I'm going to be the next Sondheim."

Alison stepped in front of him, her features grim. "We've got a problem: Brent came up to me in the hallway after English and told me I should say goodbye to you."

Jordi shrugged. "So? He's probably just jealous 'cause you'd rather hang around with me."

"I don't think so." Alison's voice lowered to an urgent hiss. "I think he meant 'goodbye' like…you're going away. Like he's going to *make* you go away."

Jordi laughed. "He can't make me 'go away,' Alison. If he tries anything else, he'll get suspension…and then *he'll* be the one going away, not me. Don't worry about it."

"Just…be careful; okay?"

Jordi gave Alison a playful toss of his head and answered, "I can handle myself, sistah girl."

Jordi stayed up most of the night, finishing *Hunchback*. He wrote of the attempted murder of Captain Phoebus, Esmeralda's would-be lover, by Frollo, and of how the gypsy was framed for the murder. He wrote of Quasimodo's daring rescue of Esmeralda from the gallows, of how he carried her back to the safety of the great cathedral, where he protected her from the King's men. He penned a song for the villainous Frollo, who tried to explain himself to Quasimodo after turning Esmeralda over to the soldiers, and who was finally killed by the enraged hunchback. And he wrote his climactic aria, as Quasimodo, too late to rescue Esmeralda a second time, sings to her corpse and consigns himself to a slow death beside her.

He knew some of it was clumsy, the melodies repetitive, the lyrics sometimes forced…but there was time to polish it later, all the time in the world. Right now, the sun was rising outside; and Jordi, not at all tired, still energized, beamed in pride. Overall he knew it was good, and he knew he'd get better with each new song, each new play.

It was a fine beginning to the day.

Alison filed into Math at 8:55, only to find Jordi waiting for her, grinning.

"I finished it."

"You're kidding! I thought there was still a lot left to go."

"There was…but I stayed up all night."

Alison shared the grin. "Where is it? Can I read it?"

"Not yet. There's still a little fine-tuning, but…Ally, it's really fuckin' good."

"I know it is."

Alison glanced past Jordi, and her mood soured. "Here comes Brent, and he looks…weird."

Jordi turned, and had to agree with Alison: Brent was walking across the room with his eyes fixed on Jordi, his stare unblinking and dead. He was shrugging out of his backpack as he crossed to where Jordi sat at his desk, smiling. Brent reached Jordi and held the pack before him.

"Whatup, Brent, m'man? Decide I needed some mascara to go with the lipstick?"

Brent reached into the backpack, pulled out a pistol, pointed it at Jordi, and fired twice.

Jordi felt an impact like a boulder crashing into him. He felt the explosions in his chest; he knew he'd been shot, and he knew he was falling. Time slowed to a crawl, and it took so long—hours—for his body to collide with the cold schoolroom floor. And yet he thought about Alison—was she next? Then he saw Alison kneeling beside him, as Brent was walking calmly out of the classroom, the gun no longer in his hand.

"Jordi—oh God, Jordi—"

Breathing was an agony; every breath felt like shards of glass piercing his lungs. He knew Alison's hands were on him, and he knew she was trying to save him.

But the cold was starting to set in; his vision was blurring around the edges.

He tried to speak, and felt blood around his tongue. "Shouldn't…end like this."

Alison started to cry as she kept the pressure on his wounds.

"It's not going to end, Jordi, it's not…"

He realized she didn't know what he was trying to say: the hunchback wasn't supposed to die in Esmeralda's arms.

Or had he really been Esmeralda all along? Then he knew: He'd been all of them—Quasimodo and Esmeralda and Frollo and Phoebus. He'd led so many lives.

He smiled at that and closed his eyes.

MONSTERS
of L.A.

DRACULA

"Fuck you, Moss, fuck the crew, and fuck this whole mov-
ie!" shrieked Dracula as he stalked off the set.

The entire crew of fifty stood in stunned silence for a few seconds, then the first assistant director, a serious young woman named Yvette, walked up to the director, Darryl Moss, and asked, "Do you want me to go after him, or—"

Moss shouted at her, "No; fuck that Eurotrash cocksucker! He's never believed in this picture. Besides, sun's almost up anyway. Let's just wrap."

Yvette turned away and shouted (as if the entire crew hadn't just heard Moss) "Okay, people, that's a wrap. We're back tomorrow night at 8 p.m."

The cameramen and gaffers, sound recorders, makeup and wardrobe people, general gophers, and the actors all grumbled and started to disperse.

One young man didn't move. He stood in the middle of the set (which supposedly depicted the hero's high-tech-and-yet-Gothic underground lair) and allowed his perfect lips to curl into a slight smirk. The director noticed and approached.

"Hey, Eddie, man—I'm sorry. That scene would've been

great if Count Prick could've remembered his lines…"

The handsome young man shook his coiffed hair, letting a single curl fall across one eye. "It's okay, Darryl. The guy's a legend…"

"A legendary pain in the ass, you mean. They warned me about him, but—Jesus, I didn't think he'd be this bad."

Eddie slapped his director's shoulder. "Aw, we'll get through this okay, man; and the movie will kick ass."

Moss grinned. "You're a great kid, Eddie."

The kid laughed.

Dracula stalked the length of his trailer, shouting into his smart phone. "Johnny, you gotta get me off this fucking movie. The script keeps getting dumber, and I don't care how many fucking Independent Spirit Awards this director has won, he's an idiot—"

The man on the other end of the phone cut Dracula off. "Drac, listen to me: Darryl Moss is not an idiot. And Eddie Cee is the hottest young actor in Hollywood right now—"

"Kid's just another vapid pretty boy. Look, how long have we been together, Johnny?"

Johnny sighed. "You know that's a loaded question, bro." Johnny's great-great-great-great grandfather, Jonathan Harker, had been Dracula's real estate agent; and now Johnny was his talent agent. It felt like five lifetimes to Johnny, even though he was only 32.

"I'm just saying—don't bullshit me, okay? I know we took this film only because nobody else would pay me what I'm worth."

There was a long pause on the other end. Finally Dracula asked, "Did I lose you?"

"No, I'm here. It's just that question of what you're worth… well, I've got some bad news, I'm afraid, Drac. I've been trying to figure out how to break it to you."

Dracula stopped pacing and stared at the phone. "WHAT?"

"Mina's asking for more money."

Dracula had to restrain an urge to hurl the phone down and grind it into fragments beneath his black leather boots. "That bitch! She already fucking cleaned me out in the divorce settlement! How can she ask for more?!"

"She claims you've missed three alimony payments in a row."

"Three…?" Dracula rubbed his forehead and thought. Hadn't he told his accountant…something? He was so angry he couldn't remember what it'd been. "Fuck. Okay, look: tell that bitch her goddamn blood money is coming."

There was a snicker on the other end. "Blood money. That's funny, Drac."

"Johnny —!"

"Okay. I'll take care of it."

Glancing up, Dracula saw a thin ray of violet light forcing its way inside the trailer. "Aw, shit, sun's coming up."

"Got it. Later man. And just try to finish up the movie, will ya?"

"Fuck you, Johnny."

Dracula ended the call and rushed to the door. Outside, his special limo with the blacked-out windows awaited him…and so did his costar, Eddie Cee. In fact, Eddie stood just a few feet away, smiling as Dracula rushed to the car, trying not to stare at the lightening sky.

"What the fuck are you looking at?" Dracula called as his chauffeur (whom he liked to refer to as Renfield, even though the man's name was Tyrone Kolodji) opened the limo door.

Eddie waved. "Oh, nothing, Mr. Dracula. See you tomorrow."

Dracula paused long enough to shoot the kid a glare of pure venom—a look that had caused dozens of mortal hearts to freeze in terror—but Eddie Cee just smiled languidly. Mildly perplexed but more concerned about the rising sun, Dracula ducked into the limo and settled back gratefully into the dark leather seats and the arms of the pretty blonde extra Renfield had chosen for him. The girl stared at him now in near-apoplectic adoration and squealed. "Omigod, it's you, it's really you! Mr. Dracula, I am your biggest fan—"

"Then be quiet." Dracula fixed the girl with a hypnotic suggestion, and her jaws fell slack. As the limo pulled away from the studio, Dracula forgot about everything else as he sank his teeth into the soft flesh of the extra's throat.

The movie was called *Coldblooded*, and starred Dracula as a vigilante hero who could move through the night unseen in pursuit of the badasses who'd killed his wife. It was a far cry from *Chamber Music*, the story of a man with a rare disease surviving the Holocaust, which had won Dracula an Oscar nomination; but *Coldblooded* was still a paycheck, and at 12 million, a reasonably decent paycheck at that. With castles to pay for, lawsuits to settle, and a vindictive ex-wife to appease, Dracula needed all the decent paychecks he could get. Sometimes he wished that moron Van Helsing really had staked him, instead of pissing himself and fleeing in terror. Hollywood had provided a luxurious sanctuary, and he liked being a movie star, but…he often wished for the old days when those who'd angered him found themselves impaled on a twelve-foot stake in his courtyard.

Three nights later, Dracula was in his trailer, languidly sucking on a brunette, when there was a knock on the door.

"Fuck off," Dracula called, before returning to the hypnotized ingénue.

"It's Eddie, Mr. D. You know—your costar? Can we talk?"

Thinking this might be a chance to dress down the young buck, Dracula responded, "Just a minute."

He grabbed a gauze pad from the stack on the trailer counter, pressed it to the girl's neck and told her, "GO."

Without so much as a blink (or bothering to pull her blouse back up) she mechanically moved to the door, opened it, and walked past Eddie Cee, who stared after her. "Was that girl… uh…?"

"Yes. Now, what can I do for you, Mr. Cee?"

"Can I come in?"

Dracula stepped back and gestured. "Please."

Eddie Cee entered and looked around. The trailer had a plasma television, Wii game set, fully stocked bar, and leather-upholstered furnishings.

Eddie whistled. "Nice crib, Dee. Way better than mine."

"Then you need a better agent, kid."

The gorgeous young actor smiled and shook his head. "Been thinking that very thing."

They locked eyes for a while, and Dracula considered hypnotizing the kid—maybe he could get him to do something incredibly stupid—but he remembered the talk he'd had with the producer yesterday (actually the producer had screamed at him until Dracula got that he was close to being fired, bye-bye twelve mil) and decided to be good. "So, Eddie, talk to me."

Eddie dropped into one of the leather chairs and clasped his hands between his knees. "It's that scene we shot before the break—the one with you and me talking about how you saved my ass, pulled me out of the gutter and fixed me up…"

"Right. What about it?"

"Well, Dee—you did a pretty spectacular job of upstaging me throughout that scene. I mean, that whole business where you reloaded the gun so they couldn't cut away from you…"

Dracula shrugged. "I'm an actor, kid."

"See, that's the thing: so am I. I'm classically trained, man; I did *Lear* for my final year in college, and I fucking *rocked.*" Eddie was getting angry now, and he didn't try to hide it; he rose slowly until he towered over Dracula. "So don't assume that just because you think I'm some dumb 'kid' that I don't know *every* trick you're pulling, *old man.* Comprende?"

Dracula felt his ancient blood boil, and he rose to match the kid's height, turning the full fury of his gaze on his youthful opponent. "Don't you talk to me like that, boy. I know more about acting than you will *ever* know. I studied with Max Reinhardt. I've eaten with Henry Irving. Jesus fucking Christ, I saw the first performance of *Lear!*"

The kid was completely unimpressed; no cowering, not even a glimmer of fear. As Dracula stared in perplexity, Eddie laughed at him—no mortal had *ever* laughed at him!—and leaned forward until he was only an inch from Dracula. "Yeah,

yeah, yeah, and you drove the Ottomans out of your country, and you were there with Napoleon on the battlefield, and you knew Robin Hood, and blahblahblah, we've heard all this bullshit a thousand times before, and it's like you, Drac — it's *old*."

Dracula was momentarily stunned. When he could speak again, he only managed, "I never said I knew Robin Hood."

"Whatever. Look, the point is: don't you fucking *ever* think you can upstage me again, asshole, because I am stronger than you think; and you better believe me when I say that you do *not* want to fuck with me."

Eddie strode out, slamming the trailer door behind him. Dracula stared after him, a thousand possibilities roiling in his mind: How had Eddie resisted him? A designer drug? A New Age brain booster? Or was it possible that Eddie wasn't human?

If that was the case…what was he?

Dracula had to know.

Three nights later, they were set to film a big action scene and the denouement for Eddie's character, who would die in a hail of bullets.

Just before the scene was to shoot, Dracula hypnotized the prop man, handed him a fistful of live bullets, and told him to load the gun. He did.

The scene was set up. The cameras were placed and ready to roll. Darryl called, "Action!" The guns fired, and Eddie's body jerked from the impact. Dracula stood just out of frame, watching and grinning as Eddie's chest erupted.

"Cut!" called Darryl. He leapt from his chair and rushed

toward Eddie, who stood staring down at his bloody chest. "You okay?"

Eddie wavered for a moment, then looked up with a grin. "I'm great! Excellent blood squibs. Do we need to go again?" Then he turned, stared at Dracula, reached into the tattered remains of his costume, plucked out a real bullet, and dropped it at Dracula's feet.

For the first time in at least a century, Dracula felt fear.

Two nights later, Dracula finished for the night at just after 3 a.m. and was approached by a scrumptious young girl on the way to his trailer. She looked at him with half-lidded eyes and bared her neck. It was all he needed. He brought her into the trailer and closed the door. Something seemed…different about the trailer, but the girl smiled and said she'd dreamed about this her whole life, and Dracula forgot all about the trailer. He sank his fangs into her luscious, yielding skin…

And dawn was breaking.

He felt a jolt of alarm struggling to break through into his consciousness. Some blanketed part of him realized time had passed, but he hadn't known how much. He felt slow and stupid. He felt…

Drugged. The girl had been on something, and it had seeped into his veins with her blood.

He staggered to his feet, stumbling past the unconscious (or dead? he didn't really care) girl to the door of the trailer. He threw it back and winced—the sky was pink. Surely the sun would rise any second.

No matter—his limo would protect him. Dracula started

to walk toward the limo…

Gone. The limo was nowhere to be seen.

"That's right, asswipe—your big fancy car is gone. It was amazing how easy it was to buy off your chauffeur; guess he's as tired of your bullshit as everyone else is."

Dracula's dulled awareness sought out the voice, and found it as Eddie Cee strolled forward, a half-smile slanting his perfect lips.

"What the…?" Dracula stood in confusion for a moment. He felt something brush his arm, and saw it was the girl stumbling past him.

"You need me anymore, Eddie?" she asked.

Eddie leaned down and gave her a small kiss. "No, baby—thanks."

Dracula stared, stunned…until the first ray of sunlight shot between two of the soundstages. He yelped and ducked back into the trailer. He could still be safe there: he had a space under the bed in the back, lined with his native soil—

"Uh-uh. 'Fraid not." That was Eddie Cee, leaping past him into the trailer. "This is going to be *my* trailer now, Dee, so I cleaned all that nasty dirt out. Oh, and—" Eddie reached for a switch in the wall, flicked it, and parts of the roof retracted, allowing lethal sunlight to intrude. "I had skylights installed."

Dracula knew now what was different about the trailer, and he would have known last night had he not been seduced and drugged by Eddie's floozy.

Panicked, Dracula fled past Eddie out of the trailer—and right into the glow of the morning sun. He shrieked and recoiled as he began to sizzle.

"You won't get away with this," he managed to gasp out, as Eddie joined him outside, stepping to the side to lounge in shade, mocking Dracula's agonies.

"But I will, Dee. The studio knows about it, and they were all for it. Of course the official report will call it an accident, one that was bound to happen sooner or later…"

Dracula writhed, but still shot Eddie a withering glance. "That's bullshit. The movie's not even done yet."

"True, but ya know what, Drac? Darryl was more than happy to rewrite it, so I'm now the hero and *you're* the one who dies in a hail of bullets. A little bit of CGI, and nobody will ever know."

Dracula watched, stricken, as his right hand—held up to shield his face from the deadly sun—turned to ash and crumbled away. His long life was ending, and he only had one last question he needed to ask, "What are you?"

Eddie chuckled and pushed away some of the ash with the toe of his expensive sneakers. "God, Dee, you're such an idiot. I'm *you*, moron! That's right! Vampire, bloodsucker, whatever."

Dracula felt his legs vanish, but at least his final thought would be a pleasing one. "Then…you'll…die with me…"

Eddie just laughed, then stepped out of shadow into the morning sun.

And sparkled.

MONSTERS
of L.A.

THE
BRIDE

THE BRIDE

"Hey, didja hear about ol' Frankenstein, how he offed him-self with a knife? Made a helluva mess, I guess."

Lizzie gaped as shock wrenched her. Her friend Angel, con-fused by the response, added, "Y'know, the old crippled vet guy hangs out around the—"

"I know who he is." Lizzie cut her off as the impact co-alesced into disbelief. "He's dead?"

Angel nodded. "Graff was the one found him. Said he'd sawed through most of his last leg, slit open his stomach, and was working on his throat when he died. Blood was fuckin' everywhere."

Lizzie's legs went out from under her, and she slid, unfeel-ing, uncomprehending, down the dirty brick wall of the bar behind her. Angel's eyes widened, and she bent down to her friend.

"Hey, honey, are you okay?"

Lizzie wanted to scream at her—"No, goddamn you, I'm not okay, because that was Danny"—but instead she sat, star-ing, trying to resolve the grief and guilt threatening to consume her.

Danny…her Danny…she hadn't seen him in ten years, since she'd told him she was leaving, going back home to get the rest of her life back together. He'd been a good man, a kind and loving man, who'd been dealt one long, continuous bad hand; he didn't move well, and two thoughts in his mind often wouldn't connect, but he'd never beaten her, he'd wanted to marry her, and he'd tried to take care of her, scrounging bottles and cans and paper from sunrise to sunset. And for a while she'd thought life was better with him, but then she'd realized it still wasn't enough, and Danny had gone as far as he would ever go. So she'd left one day, just made the decision and was gone. She was going home to Tucson, but somehow she hadn't realized how much the bus ticket would be, and there wasn't enough money, and she'd figured just a few tricks would do it. She could stand another week of fast sex with men who didn't know her name if it would get her out of this city and back to her sister in Arizona…

And then her sister had told her she didn't want to see her, and drugs made it easier to suck off another client in a car, and that had been ten years ago. She knew that what kept her from seeing Danny again wasn't ambition or regret, but shame.

It was too late now anyway, because her friend had just told her Danny was dead, that he'd killed himself.

"I should've been there," she said, between tears she hadn't known she was crying.

Angel stepped back, as if Lizzie's grief could be contagious. "Oh fuck, hon, I didn't know you knew him…"

A car stopped by the sidewalk, a man inside beckoning Angel. "Hey, look, I gotta go…I'll check on you later, okay?"

Lizzie waved her off, glad to be alone.

After a while she stopped sobbing. It was chilly for May in L.A., and the sidewalk was cold through the denim of her jeans. She rose, straightened her sequined jacket and dabbed at her face, then started along the sidewalk. She had no destination in mind, but any motion was better than sitting on cold cement, frozen even more by memories.

She tired of walking and paused, lounging by a lamppost. Thoughts of Danny (dying alone, bleeding out under a freeway, leaving a mess to be rinsed down a drain) nearly overwhelmed her, so she didn't see the white car pull up beside her. The passenger window rolled down and a handsome older man leaned across the front seat. "You look like you need some help…"

Lizzie's business instincts clicked into automatic (as they did whenever a car stopped nearby) and she bounced the hair of her wig and strutted up to the open window. "Maybe I can help *you*, sugar."

The man's eyes roamed over her quickly; she knew she was aging, but drugs had kept her thin, and the wig and clothes helped. And at least she still had all of her teeth.

The man didn't smile, but he did unlock the door, and she climbed in. As he drove off, he said, "Twenty bucks for a blow job."

Lizzie was about to engage in the usual and expected haggling—more money, restrictions on what she wouldn't do, how much he'd have to pay if he wanted those things—when she took a really good look at him, and it silenced her.

She knew him instantly. She'd last seen him eleven years ago. Danny had always spoken of the surgeon who'd put him back together, so Lizzie had sought Dr. Victor out. She'd gone to see him, begged him to help Danny, just as he'd helped before. Dr. Victor had heard her out, then handed her some free samples of painkillers and told her it was all he could do.

She'd left the meeting understanding why Danny had hated him.

"Did you hear me? Twenty bucks for a blow job?"

Lizzie forced herself to nod. "I heard. I know an alley where we won't be bothered." She gave him directions.

As she finished, she glanced down in the well between the seats and saw a chain there, with two rectangles dangling. She knew, and yet she picked them up to confirm the suspicion.

Moss, DANIEL

"These dog tags…"

Victor glanced over. "Yes. A man whose life I saved gave those to me."

Lizzie looked down at the name imprinted into the metal, and she knew: Danny—Frankenstein—a chance encounter with Victor, anger and the tags torn away and given to Victor; and Danny, reminded of what he was and would always be, had had enough and ended it all, in the only way he could think of that would mean he couldn't be put back together. He'd gotten a good, sharp knife and had set about obliterating himself.

Victor pulled into the alley and parked, then slid his seat back and unzipped his fly. "Well?"

Lizzie, without thinking, reached into her bag to get the baby wipes. She reached into his pants, cleaned him off, felt him harden immediately.

As she set her purse aside, she was glad that she still had all of her teeth.

"This is for Danny," she said as she lowered her head.

MONSTERS
of L.A.

THE
MUMMY

THE MUMMY

Hillarie Dulac stepped out of her sparkling silver convertible Jaguar XK and accepted the ticket from the valet. She strode to the sidewalk and watched as her car disappeared around the corner, hoping the idiot wouldn't let the paint job get scratched or dented. Her husband Darren was always furious when that happened.

Sighing, Hillarie turned and looked at the building front before her. There was no signage, no window, no address; the only indication that Hillarie was at the right place was a tiny engraved plaque set into the elegant stone above a buzzer.

The Nile.

She pressed the buzzer, and almost immediately the ornate wooden door swung back. "Good afternoon, Mrs. Dulac," chirped a young female voice with a slight accent.

Hillarie removed her Moss Lipow sunglasses and stepped in. The interior was unexpected after the featureless building front: the spacious reception area was painted a soothing buff color and featured built-in fountains surrounded by potted papyrus plants.

"Welcome to *The Nile*, Mrs. Dulac. I'm Titi."

Hillarie eyed the girl closely now and nearly gasped: Titi was no more than 19 or 20 and breathtakingly beautiful, with skin the color of rich wood, black hair and eyes, and a flawless body. The girl wore a simple, belted white tunic and a surprising amount of gold jewelry and makeup.

"Thank you. I must say, I'm intrigued. For one thing, my friend Nycole recommended you so highly…"

Titi smiled, and the effect was so dazzling that Hillarie was both entranced and envious. "Oh, yes, Mrs. Glissman is one of our favorite clients."

"I assume you only take new clients via recommendation? I'd never heard of you, and your entrance isn't exactly well marked…"

"We believe that security and privacy are part of what makes our treatments so special. In fact, shall we get you started?"

Titi held out a hand, indicating a hallway that led out of the lobby; and Hillarie followed her lead. A few doors down was a simple changing room, with chair, dresser, mirror, folded robe and towels, and private bath. "I'll wait outside while you change."

"Thank you Titi."

Hillarie entered the room, closed the door, and began removing her clothing. When she reached her bra and panties, she hesitated; usually she had no such qualms, but something about Titi and the vibe here unnerved her. What if they were foreign and she offended them? Then she decided that was silly—at what she (or rather Darren) was paying them, she shouldn't care if they were offended. It would be the most expensive full body wrap she'd ever had, but Nycole—who'd had (if possible) even more types of treatments than Hillarie—said it took ten years off, so Hillarie was willing to try it.

After all, she was running out of options.

She was only 39, and most would have guessed ten years younger, but age was starting to work its insidious erosion on her. She spent two hours every day working out, had a personal trainer and her own nutritionist, and had undergone everything from Botox and Lipoplasty to hot stone massage to seaweed wraps…but her limbs were starting to take on that ropy look that she saw in the rail-thin older women at the Beverly Hills restaurants and shops. She knew Darren would never divorce her (or at least not for another few years) but she was looking at her future and imagining Darren Dulac, CEO of one of the nation's biggest insurance companies, still showing off his sagging, chicken-necked wife in another ten years.

She couldn't do it.

She wrapped the linen robe about her and opened the door to find Titi handing her a steaming mug of something with an unusual smell. "What's this?"

"Our own special tea, which we brew with tana leaves imported from Egypt. It's an essential part of our treatment, and will leave you feeling relaxed and peaceful."

Hillarie wasn't entirely sure about the odd scent, but since it was an "essential," she sipped the drink. It left her tongue slightly numb, but she did instantly feel tranquil and warm.

"This way, Mrs. Dulac."

She followed Titi a short distance to another room, where two men waited. Both the room and the men were strange: the former held a huge table in the center and shelves of large jars against one wall, and the latter had shaved heads, naked chests, jewelry, tattoos, and intense stares.

"Would you finish the tea, please?"

Hillarie downed the rest of the mug's contents and began

to waver. "Tana leaves, did you say…?"

Titi leapt forward and grabbed the mug just before Hillarie dropped it. "That's right, Mrs. Dulac. It affects most of our clients that way. Now I'm just going to help you out of your robe…"

Hillarie let Titi unbelt the robe and slip it from her shoulders. She dimly recalled her hesitation of a few moments earlier, but—even though she stood in front of two half-naked men—her anxieties had all fled.

The two men stepped forward now, and placed a large vat of some solution on the table, then began using brushes to apply the thick liquid to Hillarie's skin, as Titi held her steady.

"Oh, what's this?"

"It's for exfoliation—a salt called natron that we import directly from the banks of the Nile River."

Hillarie giggled. "Oh, that's where you get your name!"

"Yes."

"Are you all Egyptian?"

A strange look passed between the two silent men and Titi. "Yes," Titi finally answered, "we are, although we've been in this country for a long time now."

"Oh, please," Hillarie said, eyeing the gorgeous girl, "how long can you have been *anywhere*?"

"Well, Mrs. Dulac, I've had this treatment, and I'm really much older than I look."

"Oh. Well, that's impressive." Hillarie wasn't sure she believed it, but she hoped it was true.

The men brushed the solution over her entire body below the neck, and as it began to dry, Hillarie felt it start to harden.

"Now, let's get you on the table before that completely sets."

The two men guided Hillarie onto the table, laying her

back across carefully positioned cloth strips; they posed her as Titi explained the process.

"Now, Mrs. Dulac, we're going to commence with the wrap. You might be interested to know that our wrapping is made from the finest imported Egyptian linen. We'll start at the feet."

Working quickly and with obvious experience, the two men began wrapping the strips around Hillarie, first binding her feet and legs together, then rolling her easily from side to side to wrap her hips and torso.

The tea seemed to be working more on Hillarie now, and she abruptly realized that Titi was saying something to her. "I'm sorry…what?"

"I just wanted to let you know that we'll be doing your arms now."

By the time she'd processed that sentence, the two men had nearly finished with her arms individually, and then a final layer wrapped her arms to her sides. Hillarie had a brief, alarming thought—she was completely helpless now—but the pleasant haze brought on by the tea quickly doused her concerns.

"So how long do I stay in this?"

Titi glanced at the two men, and Hillarie didn't like her smile. "Oh, quite some time, Mrs. Dulac. But you won't even notice."

"How long? And why won't I notice?"

Titi now bent down over Hillarie and spoke to her urgently. "Aren't you here because you want to look young? Because you're desperately afraid that your wealthy husband will dispose of you the instant he realizes that there's a better, newer model available?"

Hillarie could barely whisper an answer. "Yes."

"Well, trust me, Mrs. Dulac: You are going to stay young now *forever*. That's why our treatment is so exclusive, and so expensive."

"Forever? That's not exactly accurate…"

Titi laughed. "I'd call three-thousand, five-hundred and sixty years reasonably close to 'forever'."

"What are you talking about?"

"Mrs. Dulac," the girl said, with an edge of pride in her voice, "my full name is Nefertiti. You might have heard of me."

Hillarie ran the name through her dulled brain until she came up with something: an Egyptian queen, a famous sculpture…

She laughed. The tea seemed to make everything light. "Of course. And now you work in a spa in Beverly Hills."

"Truthfully, Mrs. Dulac…we're a little more than a spa. We think of ourselves as a center for preserving traditional practices. And we do love wealth."

Nefertiti nodded at the two men. One stepped forward, holding some sort of long, narrow tool with a small hook on one end. He began to bend over Hillarie.

"What's that for?"

"Well, Mrs. Dulac, this is the only part of the treatment that might be slightly uncomfortable. You see, we use this to poke a hole in the ethmoid bone at the top of the nasal cavity, and then we use it to remove the brain."

Alarm now penetrated Hillarie's drug fog, and she started to squirm, but realized that the natron and the linen bandages held her firmly in place. Her eyes widened as the tool was lowered toward her face. "You won't get away with this. People know where I am today. Nycole knows—"

"Please, Hillarie—Nycole Glissman is already ours. We'll

soon control nearly every woman in Beverly Hills, and that means we'll control a considerable amount of this nation's money."

Hillarie could only scream as she felt the thin, cold metal slide into her nose.

MONSTERS
of L.A.

THE INVISIBLE
WOMAN

THE INVISIBLE WOMAN

Have you ever come home to find your front door swinging open? I've heard people use the word "violated" to describe the way they feel. I don't know…it's both more and less than that. You slowly push the door open, and you take that first step in, and your heart's pounding — then it stops dead when you see everything that's gone. And it was almost everything. Not that I had much to begin with, but these guys even took some of my clothes. I think that bothered me more than the TV.

I lived on the third floor of a three-story building — I thought that'd be safer, you know? — but they'd come down from the roof. They'd used a crowbar to smash in one window. It was during the day, and nobody heard anything. One neighbor thought she'd seen somebody leaving, but she couldn't seem to remember what he'd looked like. They'd walked right out the front door. Considering how much was gone, I figured there were either a couple of them, or one guy making trips. Here's the ironic part, another one of life's little bad jokes: they left their crowbar — the one they used to smash in my window with — and there were big grimy-black fingerprints on the wall by the door. I called the police, thinking this'd be open and shut. I was right—except the door shut on me. It wasn't an emergency, they said, so the cops didn't arrive until a day later. When I showed them all the evidence, they just sighed and asked if I wanted to file a report. I couldn't believe it—did I want to file a report?! They said chances were practically nil that the guys who'd robbed me would ever be caught. When they left, they didn't even take the crowbar. I put it aside for a few days, thinking for some reason they might come back for it. Finally I realized that was never gonna happen, so I put it in my car. It's a good one, too. Probably worth more than some of what they took.

After that I started to notice things. Lots of things. I heard a woman in a line at the grocery store talk about how she found a man breaking into her car, and when she confronted him, he just smiled and walked away. Not ran, but walked. Someone in a post office rattled on about a homeless guy who woke up on the sidewalk one morning to find himself in the process of being beaten by the local store owner, and the police responded instantly—to cart the homeless guy off. Late one night at a fast food place I watched two men open the trunk of their car, pull out a hand to check on a pulse, then put the hand back and close the cover. I didn't bother to call the police.

All this was putting an idea into my head, an idea I couldn't shake, that just grew stronger and stronger: you could get away with anything, the bigger the easier, as long as you stayed low and didn't step on the wrong toes. I mean, *anything.* Take me, for instance: If I did do something the police gave a shit about, would they ever look at someone like me as a suspect? Thirty-something, female, plain-looking, single and childless, spotless record, not so much as a parking ticket. I was virtually invisible. I could go anywhere, do anything, and no one would notice. I began sensing a new spirit within myself, one I'd never known before: power. I could get away with anything, I was sure. But I wouldn't use my new knowledge for small gain. No; I'd store it, an account collecting interest, steady and growing.

For a long time I didn't use it. I just let stuff wash over me, knowing nothing could touch me. Sometimes I dreamed about—doing things. Like the next time the guy below me cranked his stereo at two in the morning, I'd go down and drive an ice pick into one ear. I thought about getting passed over for another raise, then going in to hold a gun on the boss until he begged to give me a promotion; and I shot him anyway. As I said, I was just banking time. But it wasn't until that night with my father that I cashed the account in.

Once a month I helped Dad out with his paperwork—he needed it since he'd had that stroke. He didn't have anyone else—my mother had left us both fifteen years ago—and I always went, although I didn't know why. But tonight...it was the first time I'd seen him since my big change. He was watching a boxing match when I got there. He opened the door, didn't say anything, just went back to his TV I started to look at his stroke medicine, the new full vial of pills sitting there by the sink. Every night he drank three or four beers before dinner—even though his doctors had told him to cut back; he gulped down the Buds so fast he didn't have time to taste them. So tonight I just walked into the kitchen, picked up the pills, the beers and a paper towel, and told him I was taking the trash out. I went out to the garage, dumped the whole vial into the towel, wrapped it up and smashed it with that crowbar until it was powder. When I got back he was screaming bloody murder about his beer. He had no idea how right he was. Just chugged it like always.

He was dead forty minutes later.

I just watched the whole thing, then called 911 and the paramedics came. They tried CPR, then loaded him into the ambulance. I followed. At the hospital an overworked doctor pronounced it massive coronary failure and asked if I wanted an autopsy. I looked appropriately bewildered and said no. That was it. No cops, no suspicious detective dogging my every move, like in some bad thriller; they don't have time in L.A. to investigate every seventy-year-old stroke patient who keels over dead. I kept the empty pill bottle as a souvenir.

If I'd felt powerful before, now I felt...invulnerable. Because now I knew I was right. My invisibility had worked. I'd killed the bastard, and I think in his last few moments he even knew it was me, maybe even saw me...maybe. But, like I'd guessed, no one else did. They didn't look at me; they didn't even look through me.

I wondered what it would be like—well, if I'd done it once...The second time started a few nights later, when I was driving on the freeway. A fucked-up little teenybopper cut me off, then flipped me off. Before I really knew it, I was following her off the freeway and through upper-class suburbia in the hills at one end of the San Fernando Valley. My invisibility held, because when she pulled into a driveway and got out, she obviously had no idea I was parked a house away, watching. When she went in she had to turn on all the lights, so I knew she was alone. She wasn't much bigger than I was; she was a stupid drunk kid, and I still had the crowbar. I felt its weight in my hand and imagined how it would feel when I drove it into her head, smashing the skull like a party piñata. I wondered if there'd be a struggle, if she'd have the necessary breath to scream, if she'd live long enough for me to tell her why. I wondered what her parents would say when they found her, if her daddy would yell, "You see? I knew she was worthless, that she'd end up like this!" Would he remember how he'd locked her in the closet when she'd burned his best shirt with the iron? Or when he'd gone away for two weeks when she was ten, leaving her alone with twenty dollars and no phone number? Would he think about all the times he'd laughed and told his friends, children shouldn't be seen or heard?! About the times he—

My fingers hurt. I was standing on the sidewalk in front of the house, holding the crowbar so hard my knuckles were bled white. It was a while later, because the house lights were out and her car was gone. Had I been standing there when the girl had left again, or was I in the car? Had she seen me at all? When I got back in the car, I glanced into the rearview mirror—and there was no one there. I looked hard, but there was just...nothing. Nothing but an empty car. Now I'm invisible even to myself.

I think maybe...I think I'm tired of being invisible. It's been long enough. I don't want this any more. This power, invisibility. I want...something new.

How do I make anyone see me again?

MONSTERS
of L.A.

THE MAD
SCIENTIST

THE MAD SCIENTIST

Dr. West looked down once at the woman on the metal ta-
ble, waited until the others left the room, then set up a laptop
at the head of the table. Once the laptop was functioning, he
opened his foam-padded case and removed a full syringe.

"Now," he said, addressing the prone woman, "I know I
don't have to explain the basics of nanotechnology to you, since
we've been over it so many times. As you know, I've personally
led a team that has conducted multiple successful tests on mice,
but this is the first test on a human subject. I'm going to record
a few notes while we proceed, given the possible historical sig-
nificance of this procedure."

The woman didn't respond.

Dr. West took that as agreement, and used his other hand
to lay out a voice-activated digital recorder. He turned it on,
then returned his attention to the syringe, which contained an
inch of milky fluid.

"Today we'll be injecting 10,000 nanorobots functioning
as cell repair machines, and an additional 10,000 nanobiophar-
maceuticals. All nanoparticles have been designed with specific functions, and should achieve complete biodistribution

through the circulatory system in ten seconds. I will be controlling certain functions, recording incoming data, and imaging through my laptop."

Inhaling deeply, Dr. West paused for a moment, containing his excitement; then he placed the needle tip of the syringe against a vein on the woman's left arm. "We'll begin. You'll feel a small sting, but it shouldn't be any worse than a regular shot. You shouldn't feel anything after that for a few seconds, then there may be a few strange sensations as the nanorobots move to their targeted areas and begin cellular repair."

He depressed the plunger, set the hypodermic aside, swabbed the small prick on his patient's arm, and immediately turned his attention to the laptop screen, which was alight with motion.

"We're getting good, solid imaging, exactly what I expected...the first group is now approaching the aortic valve..."

Dr. West made the mistake, then, of glancing up and seeing the patient's face, and he was nearly staggered by a wave of grief, of shock...the things he'd been experiencing for the last four hours, since he'd been given the news. But he pushed those thoughts aside and focused instead on his tasks.

"Patient will be requiring traditional surgery as well, mainly for cosmetic repair to areas of the face, but that is not our immediate concern."

The woman's body jumped, and Dr. West gasped. The laptop screen showed intense activity, and Dr. West had to clutch the edges of the table to stay upright. "My God, the repair is proceeding even more quickly than my best estimations—"

He broke off as her chest hitched. After a few small convulsions, it returned to normal activity.

"Recording pulse now at 50 b.p.m. and rising. Blood pressure is 80 over 50 and rising..."

The woman's entire body shivered, and Dr. West cried out in joy and triumph. He forgot all about the horrible phone call he'd received this morning, the one telling him about the car accident and the ambulance arriving here at Cedars-Sinai Hospital.

"Temperature is at 92.5 degrees and rising rapidly..."

He pushed aside the terrible memory of the hour-long drive up from Irvine, of being taken to the morgue, of asking for a few moments alone.

"Repair is nearly complete..."

His own heart nearly stopped as he looked down in anxious anticipation, and then overwhelming joy.

His dead wife opened her eyes.

MONSTERS
of L.A.

THE
WEREWOLF

THE WEREWOLF

Fourth Victim Suspected in Killing Spree

By the Associated Press

RENO—The partially decomposed remains of a woman was discovered Saturday afternoon by two hikers just outside Reno, Nevada.

George McMasters, 23, and Linda Antonio, 22, were following the course of a dry creek bed when they noticed what appeared to be a human hand extending above the surface of the dirt on one bank. "It looked like somebody had buried it real shallow," noted McMasters.

The pair promptly reported the grisly discovery to the county sheriff, who soon turned the case over to federal authorities. FBI Investigator Thomas Haskell confirmed that the unidentified woman's wounds bore a strong resemblance to those found on victims near Minneapolis, Chicago and Boston.

Please see WOMAN, B16

"Reno, Minneapolis, Chicago, and Boston...hey man, didn't we play all those places?"

Joe D ducked the empty Coke cans, foam coffee cups and epithets that were hurled at him by the others on the bus. "Oh, like you can remember *anywhere* we've played," Chaz the bass player taunted.

As the bantering went on, Hardy, seated alone near the front of the bus, stared out a window. The iPod headphones were limp around his neck, small sounds issuing from the gray pads on the ends. The landscape outside was changing from California desert to the first outlying of suburbia, and Hardy knew they'd be home soon.

Hardy tried to ignore the sounds, the jokes behind him. He wanted to think about the job, about returning to L.A—but his thoughts kept circling back to the newspaper article.

Reno, Minneapolis, Chicago, Boston. Yeah, they *had* played all those places, Howlin' Monck and his troop of road-ies, managers, and numerous, assorted hangers-on. At least the papers hadn't picked up on that connection yet. They also hadn't found the other three (Orlando, Atlanta, Oklahoma City) but Hardy knew they would, no matter how well he did his job. In time they would all be found, and someone would put the dates together. Hardy rolled them over in his mind: 4/6, 5/4, 6/4, 7/3, 8/2, 8/31…they ran like a Las Vegas gam-bler's lunatic bets.

He knew he would soon add a new number to the roster, that of 9/30.

Today.

Tonight.

Another full moon.

Hardy and Howlin' Monck were alone in the star's dressing room, backstage at the Sunset Strip House of Blues, thirty minutes before showtime. The cacophony of the opening band was muffled to little more than a monotonous rhythmic thump here, away from the stage. The room was windowless, but that didn't matter. Monck didn't need to be directly beneath the full moon.

Hardy handed Monck another pill and a bottle of Cuervo Gold, then stepped back, watching with his usual mix of fascination and dread.

It started as it always did: sweat broke out on Monck's skin and he trembled, as his unwashed, scraggly hair grew long and rich, his beard streamed out in undulating waves, the bones in his face subtly shifted, lengthened, strengthened.

When Hardy saw the first hint of a growing fang, he shouted, "Monck—!"

Monck blinked, then looked at Hardy in the mirror. "You're a worrier, Hardy. I'm not going to lose control."

The half-wolf laughed, but Hardy was neither amused nor frightened. "Yeah, you're right about that. I do worry, because you *like* to lose control; but you can't tonight."

Monck, satisfied that he had stopped the transformation at the right point, turned away from the mirror to take up the gleaming Fender guitar. "Fuck off, Hardy. This is L.A. What's one more guy out of control?"

"L.A.'s what worries me. It's our hometown. You don't shit where you eat…Al."

The use of his real name, of the reminder that he'd once been an ordinary kid in San Bernardino named Albert Monck, brought Monck's eyes up to Hardy's. "I'm Howlin' Monck, and you're just a roadie, you little shit—"

"No — I'm a roadie who knows everything about you, Al. Don't forget that."

"Christ, Hardy, if you want a raise, just fucking ask for it."

When Hardy didn't answer, Monck ripped off a quick arpeggio on the strings. Even without the amp, it sounded good.

"Maybe I can't stop any more," Monck murmured over a chord progression, "maybe it's all tied in with the music."

"I don't believe that. C'mon, Monck, you were the greatest fucking axeman in the world before — well, you know. You blew 'em all away. Beck, Page…even Clapton."

"You saying I don't now?"

"No," Hardy breathed out, suddenly, absurdly, feeling like crying, "but I'm saying…I'm not sure it's worth it any more."

Hardy hated himself for what he felt when he watched Howlin' Monck play. If anything, he was better now, better than he'd been back before it had happened five years ago.

It had been an encounter with a particularly lithesome London groupie, one who had left the drunk-and-passed-out Monck covered with bite marks, and increasingly anxious as the next full moon approached. After the first two times he'd disappeared, they had cancelled the rest of his '06 European tour. He'd spent a year's worth of full moons sedating himself heavily. Music insiders speculated that the brilliant young guitarist who had just started to gain a reputation, was a victim of early burnout.

Hardy had been through it all. He'd been only 15 when he'd heard Monck's first album, *Urban Vengeance*, and it had changed his life. He would never forget the first time, sitting in his friend Clay's bedroom in a tumbledown house in Sun Valley, sharing a badly rolled, damp blunt. The music had spoken to him in bold notes; the rhythms had told him he wasn't alone; the riffs had taken him to a place where he found belonging. A year later, he quit school to help a local band haul ass on a regional tour. At 17, he got hired on Howlin' Monck's road crew. They gave him his name because one of the other crewmembers had joked about what a hard-on he had for Monck's playing.

Hardy was there, in the hotel room in London, when Monck returned the morning after the first disappearance, half-naked, covered with mud and sticky-dried clots, drained from the adrenalin rush of terror. He got Howlin' the drugs that kept the madness at bay, and he stood by in Monck's bedroom at home in Malibu and watched the transformation that overtook his tranquilized idol. He had supported Monck's efforts to arrest the change, and had risked his life once a month until Howlin' had learned.

After that, Howlin' Monck's genius and popularity both exploded. The gut-wrenching howls were rumored to be recorded in the studio only on full moon nights, and fans willingly paid quadruple scalper's prices for tickets to concerts held under the orb. More than one critic had named "animal magnetism" a prime factor in Howlin' Monck's success.

…but for Hardy, it had always been the music.

He would have died to protect the music, and when Monck took to letting go after concerts, at first Hardy hadn't questioned his role as janitor to the gruesome messes.

Initially he thought something had affected Monck's control, that he truly couldn't help the violence that seized him. But then, when he heard Monck laugh about the third or fourth one, Hardy realized the truth: Howlin' Monck was indulging himself.

And the music just kept getting better.

The one in Reno had been especially bad. Hardy had driven the specially outfitted limo that had taken Monck and the chosen groupie (the carefully chosen groupie, a runaway with no family to miss her) up into the hills. He could still hear the girl's agonized, choking cries as Monck had forced his way into her, a rape that went beyond sexual. He had gutted her with his new claws as he'd climaxed, then he'd staggered off into the woods. When Hardy had climbed from behind the wheel and looked into the backseat, the girl was sprawled, legs spread, blue jeans and halter top shredded, with the thick ropes of her intestines spilling down onto the floor and out across the surrounding dirt. Hardy had gone to the trunk for the usual roll of black plastic sheeting, tape, gloves and shovels, and was pulling the girl by the ankles out onto the plastic when the unimaginable had happened.

She moaned.

He froze, one gloved hand still wrapped in a coil of gray, leaking gut; then he was assaulted by violent nausea. He swallowed it back and pulled her onto the plastic, then folded it carefully around her, taping it shut. She was gasping within, little choking sobs of horror; and Hardy hadn't realized he was screaming "Stop it!" until he felt her dead under his hands, still wrapped around her neck through the tape and plastic. Then he had vomited, a convulsive spasm that left him dry heaving and weak.

The hole was shallow and not far from the road. He'd gone back to the limo, and heard the CD still playing over the car's stereo system. It was on a song from Monck's last album, a piece called "Night on Hairy Mountain." He shut it off and waited, shivering in the front seat, until Howlin' Monck had returned at moonset. Monck was filthy but human, his eyes mad, as he curled up in the blood and bile on the leather seats and fell soundly asleep. Hardy would finish cleaning up the car later, but he knew his memories, the pictures, would be harder to dispose of.

Especially that last one of Monck: smiling, satisfied, glutted, sleeping in the remains of a young girl.

A month later, Hardy was doing it again. Parked on a lonely hill above Malibu, Monck's revels had been so violent it took Hardy an hour just to clean off the inside of the tinted rear windshield. It didn't sicken him any more; he had learned to breathe through his mouth and work quickly. But the half-smothered screams and Monck's brutish, stuttering growl—had it been a laugh?

Hardy realized that if he didn't stop this soon, there would be no more room in his head for the music.

"So what're you trying to tell me, Hardy? Huh?!"

They were in a hotel suite that Monck had rented at the Chateau Marmont, just because he didn't feel like driving another hour west to home. Monck, looking haggard, was doing lines of coke on a glass coffee table. Standing watchfully over him was Joe D, the newspaper-reading roadie who had been close to the boss a lot lately.

"You know what, Monck." He glared at Joe D, then back at Howlin'. "In private."

"Joe knows, Hardy."

When Hardy gaped, Monck snorted and went on. "Yeah, it's not your precious little secret alone any more, Hardy. So whatever the fuck you gotta say, say it in front of Joe."

Hardy shot a last glance at the impassive Joe, shaking, trying to keep his voice even. "What the fuck kind of game is this, Al?"

Monck just grinned at him.

Hardy went on. "They found the one from last night. It's gotta stop."

"Get real, man," Monck laughed, "they think they're lookin' for some fucked-up nutcase with a hungry pet doggie. They'll never connect it to us."

Hardy felt his stomach lurch. "This is not 'us' —"

Monck suddenly exploded, standing up so fast his knees sent the glass table flipping into the air to land with a deafening CRRRASSH! Even Joe flinched, uncrossing his arms and stepping backward.

"No shit?" shrieked Monck. "Who picks the girls, drives the car, digs the holes?"

Monck shoved up into Hardy's face, but Hardy didn't budge. "And I got news for ya, ya little dickwad: it's gonna keep on until I say it ends, 'cause you may be in it as deep as I am, but I'm still the one in charge."

There was a knock on the door, followed by a polite inquiry, "Mr. — uh, Howlin'? Is everything alright — ?"

Monck screamed at the door, "Fine, now clear the fuck out!"

Joe D took his cue and moved to the door, opening it slightly and dismissing the concerned party with a few words and twenties.

Monck had already turned back to find Hardy steeling himself, fixing Monck with a contemptuous glare. "You're wrong, Al. You're not in charge any more. You haven't been for a long time. I don't even think Al Monck's still in there, only Howlin's left. And he isn't human."

"You're right," Monck spat as he grabbed a classic Gibson acoustic from the couch, "he's not human. He's a god."

Hardy gaped briefly, then turned to go. At the door, he hesitated long enough to say, softly, "Funny, Howlin'—most gods don't have to do their own sacrifices."

Then he muttered, "Have fun" to Joe, and strode out, slamming the door behind him. As he walked away, he heard the sound of the Gibson being smashed repeatedly against the wall.

Howlin' Monck's triumphant U.S. tour was almost over; there was one last gig to be played, at the Greek Theatre in the Hollywood Hills, outdoors under the light of the next full moon. Hardy stayed to himself, avoiding Joe D and Monck, working the situation over in his mind. He thought about quitting, running, somewhere far away…but he knew Joe D was more than just Monck's newest confidante.

He was a replacement.

Instead, Hardy started planning for the concert; it was going to be taped live and sent via satellite to pay cable systems all over the U.S. The audience would be in the millions. Hardy knew his only worry would be the Greek's security, but he thought he could get what he needed through. It wasn't even drugs, for Christ's sake.

Just a gun.

Hardy's plan included giving Monck a last chance there at the Greek, a final confrontation before their intertwined destinies were sealed. But as Hardy approached Monck's dressing room, he saw Joe D enter first, his usually stoic face flushed with excitement.

There were two heavily muscled gangstas with him Hardy had never seen before. He knew it wouldn't be a groupie riding in the back of the limo tonight.

His heart hammering in his throat, he ran for the stage area. The opening act was done; Monck's equipment was already in place, the crowd thrumming nervously.

Hardy opted for an obscure wing of the main stage, hidden by the proscenium arch. He positioned himself there, prayed he hadn't been seen in the near-dark preshow chaos, and waited.

The show started only 30 minutes late. When Monck's eponymous howl screeched through the amps, the place erupted. Even Hardy couldn't suppress a shudder rippling his spine. Howlin' leapt onto the stage from his giant descending platform shaped like a nearly full moon, and Hardy saw instantly, with a small shock, that he had let the change go further tonight than ever before. His face was almost completely a mass of thick, coarse curls, his eyes hidden behind sunglasses.

He snapped a string with a talon.

Only Hardy—and maybe Joe D, Hardy thought bitterly—realized fully what had happened. Monck covered instantly, improvising a wild solo that almost made Hardy reconsider. Even with only five strings, even with claws instead of fingertips, there was no denying the artistry, the sheer technical virtuosity of the playing.

But when Howlin' threw a lascivious hip grind in the direction of a particularly scantily clad teen in the front row, Hardy found his motivation again. He waited until the first tune finished, Monck changed guitars, and started the second number. It was an oldie, "Dying For You."

It was the first Howlin' Monck song Hardy had ever heard.

He was crying as he stumbled to the edge of the stage. He had pushed his way out before any of the other backstage onlookers grasped what was happening. He dimly heard Joe D screaming for his hired hands. Oblivious to the band, the audience, the cameramen, the millions they represented, Hardy strode with determination up to Monck…

…who didn't stop playing until he saw the gun.

The band faltered only a second, but the drums never lost the beat, and the rest finally shrugged and went on.

Monck and Hardy locked gazes; then Monck pulled the shades off to fix Hardy with eyes that flashed phosphorescent emerald. He glanced down at the gun and hissed one word out over the thundering music, "Silver?"

Hardy, who knew the lore as well as Monck, shook his head. "Only lead."

Then Monck laughed and spread his arms wide in a gesture of pure theatricality. "You stupid shit. Kill me now and I'll just rise again at the next full moon."

Hardy fired six times, emptying the magazine.

Only when they saw Monck go down did anyone realize this was not part of the act. The crowd, of course, roared approval at this new addition to the Howlin' Monck stage extravaganza.

Within seconds, Joe D's roughs had Hardy pinned to the ground, the gun wrested from his sweating hands. A circle had formed around the fallen Monck. One man was already crying as another looked up and shouted, "Jesus, man, he's dead."

The band did stop playing then. The stage manager frantically called to the tech booth to cut the lights. The crowd screamed outrage as the stage was plunged into darkness and Monck was carried off. A moment later, Hardy was jerked to his feet and half-dragged, half-shoved into the wings, already the greatest pariah since Mark David Chapman.

Later, those who had witnessed Howlin' Monck's final concert would recall, with contempt, how his assassin had smiled as he was led to justice. And there were his legendary last words before he was turned over to the L.A.P.D.— "I stopped it. It won't matter if he comes back, because I killed the music."

Rock Star's Tomb Robbed

By the Associated Press

HOLLYWOOD—Police were called to Hollywood Forever Cemetery yesterday morning to investigate a grisly crime: the tomb of late rock star "Howlin'" Albert Monck was vandalized and the body stolen, apparently the night before.

Monck, who died last month as a result of a shooting, which occurred during a live, internationally televised concert, had requested interment in the elaborate crypt. Police are now questioning his associates, including alleged assassin William "Hardy" Martins. So far they have no clues.

The caretaker who first came upon the vandalism, Gerald Washburn, 46, commented, "I don't even know how they broke into the tomb. It was clean, like somebody had just pushed the door open."

Police are still investigating Martins' claim that Monck was a serial killer who had slain at least eight women across the U.S.

MONSTERS
of L.A.

THE HAUNTED
HOUSE

THE HAUNTED HOUSE

"Take, for example, a haunted house...wherein some one room is the scene of a ghostly representation of some long past tragedy. On a psychometric hypothesis the original tragedy has been literally photographed on its material surroundings..."
— Sir Oliver Lodge, *Man and the Universe* (1908)

The Donegan house had stood on its hill in Angelino Heights since 1888. It had been added to, divided, remodeled, forgotten, and refurbished during its long life. It had withstood time, rain, sun, earthquakes, and smog; it had sheltered young couples, families, singles, grandparents, and boarders. In its time, it had seen one natural death (second owner Millie Chautauqua, who'd died in her bed at the age of 93) one suicide (a young boarder named Charles Pace whose fiancée had jilted him, so he'd hung himself from the extravagant overhead light fixture in his room) and two messy divorces. But it had also held laughter, whispers of love, exclamations of delight, congenial gatherings, squeals of playful children, purring cats, and the sound of canine tails thumping excitedly against its doors and walls.

The house was empty now, so it slept, until that time when it would once again partner in pursuit of a great dream.

An hour before sunset, two vans pulled up into the driveway of the Donegan house, just northwest of downtown Los Angeles. The vans bore the striking logo of a television show called *Ghostmasters*.

Men with cameras stepped out of the rear vehicle, then the doors on the front van flew back dramatically and the three "Ghostmasters" leapt out, lining up to pose between the cameras and the house. The trio wore jackets emblazoned with the series logo, and backpacks and utility belts full of equipment. As they waited before the house in the late afternoon sunlight, tinged gold from the Los Angeles smog, the cameras captured the "For Sale" signs and panned across peeling paint and cracked paving stones. After a few seconds, a well-dressed, middle-aged woman stepped out of the house and greeted them.

"Hi," she said, shaking hands, "I'm Eleanor Baker, the real estate agent handling the Donegan house."

The men introduced themselves: Martin Jones was a tall, dark-haired man with the sort of gaunt features that somehow translated as handsome to a television camera; David Pulaski was stocky, with thinning blonde hair and a short beard; and Johnny Romano was barely twenty, with pierced ears and a perpetual baseball cap.

"So," Martin said, "we understand the house has been on the market for a while."

"About a year," answered Eleanor.

Martin knew the real reason was that the house was expensive and the world was in a recession, but the producers had spoken to Eleanor beforehand, and briefed her on the answers they were looking for.

Eleanor complied. "There have been reports from previous owners and potential buyers of some—disturbing activity, and that seems to be making the house a tough sell."

"It's a beautiful house," Johnny said, gazing up.

"Yes, it is. It was built in 1888 by Benjamin Donegan, who'd made a fortune in the insurance business back east and moved to Los Angeles for health reasons. Mr. Donegan and his wife ended up dying tragically in a train accident a few years later, and the house was taken over by an elderly aunt, Millie. Millie died here in 1910, and at that point the property passed through a number of owners."

David pointed to a room on the second floor. The window was curtainless, and the interior of the room, away from the sun, peered out like a dark eye. "There was a suicide here, in that room right up there…"

Eleanor nodded. "In 1938, the house was acquired by a couple who rented rooms to boarders. In 1940, a young man named Charles Pace was abandoned by his girlfriend; and he hung himself in that room."

Martin, ever mindful that the show was in its fifth season and ratings had been slipping, asked, "And there have been reports ever since of creaking sounds from that room, right?"

"Yes, and one buyer was scared away when she claimed to see the figure of a man with a bent neck, reflected in a mirror in that room."

"Full-body apparition," Johnny murmured. David nodded in agreement. Martin silently applauded.

"What else?" Martin asked.

"Well, we've had reports of a cold spot in the rear down-stairs bedroom —"

David cut her off. "— where Millie was found dead?"

"Right."

"And wasn't there a rumor of a boarder who was a witch?"

Eleanor smiled. "There was once a tenant named Martha Joosten who dabbled in some odd things…"

"Okay. Let's go in." Martin held out an arm, and Eleanor turned to lead the way, the cameras following.

The house stirred as it was entered, but this was no potential new owner hoping to fall in love, nor even a casual admirer. These men sought other rewards.

The house had felt Charles Pace's agonized final moments and knew that his grief had been so all consuming it had left nothing of the young man behind. And it had watched as ancient little Millie Chautauqua had dreamed a last dream, smiling, before her heart stopped. It knew the lie of Martha Joosten, who had made herb teas for sick friends, and nothing more.

The house, however, kept its silence and hoped the intruders would leave soon, allowing it to return to serenity.

After night fell, the Ghostmasters set up their cameras, their sound recorders, and their thermometers throughout the house. At 10 p.m., they turned out the lights and entered the house, followed by their cameramen. They used small flash-lights to find their way through the spacious, three-story abode.

They started on the ground floor, at the base of the large main staircase that rose to the upper levels.

Martin shone his light around, knowing that it would paint the house in broad swaths of high contrast black-and-white that would look appropriately stark and unsettling on high-definition televisions. "We're going to head into the rear bedroom first, since that's on the ground floor and there have been reports of a cold spot there."

The trio and the cameramen walked to the bedroom at the rear of the house. In the darkness, they passed a kitchen that loomed with shadows of cupboards and a center island, but they ignored it; they had no interest in a room that had harbored warmth and the pleasure of food. They reached the rear bedroom—a large, barren room—and David and Martin roamed the interior with handheld digital thermometers, while Johnny held out a small sound recorder.

"If anyone's here," Johnny called out, "we're friends who just want to visit. We're not here to alarm you or anger you; we'd just like to talk. If you're listening, just let us know; make a sound and we'll know."

Overhead, the ancient floorboards creaked.

"Did you hear that?" Martin called out in hushed, urgent tones, uttered with the ease of a natural actor.

"Yeah," both Johnny and David muttered. Johnny allowed a suspenseful few beats, then added, "do it again so we know it's definitely you."

The creak came again.

"We've got contact!" Johnny said, his eyes wide.

"Yeah," David answered, somewhat breathlessly.

"And guys, check this out…" Martin waved his thermometer in a circle near the ceiling. "Sixty-eight degrees…sixty-seven…sixty-five…sixty-four…we've definitely got some activity going on right here."

David nodded, then said, "Let's head upstairs to the suicide's room."

The others followed him out.

The house was angry.

Its boards were its bones; they were old and they often creaked. It knew of the cold place in the bedroom, where a space between a window and a wall, created by a small quake, had never been repaired properly. But now the house cursed its own infirmities, and waited, biding, hoping for this intrusion to end quickly.

On the way up the stairs, Martin planned.

He knew he couldn't go too far—he couldn't claim to actually see the ghost of Charles Pace, for example, or viewers would feel cheated because they hadn't witnessed the sighting. He could claim that something had touched him; that was always guaranteed to incite a stab of music and a chill in viewers at home. He'd need to make it good though, because otherwise *Ghostmasters* would be canceled at the end of the season; and Martin had no interest in returning to his previous life as a welder. He liked the money, the fame, the women.

They reached the second floor landing, and David led the way down a long hall. But he hadn't gone ten feet before he stopped, holding out his hands to halt the others.

"Did you hear that?"

Martin stopped, listening. He heard nothing but a car passing outside.

David continued. "Sounds like music."

Martin knew any music was likely to be emanating from the car, but he nonetheless nodded. "It *does* sound like music. Like…something old, from the '20s, or even earlier…"

They listened for a few beats, allowing the cameramen to capture their raised faces and tense postures. David finally shrugged. "It's gone now."

They continued down the hall until they reached the last doorway on the left. The room was similar to the one they'd visited below—an empty room with dingy paint and old wooden floorboards.

"This is it." David looked around the room. "This is where Charles Pace hung himself."

Martin gestured at the lighting fixture in the center of the room. It was obviously no more than twenty years old and couldn't possibly have supported the weight of a body, but that didn't matter when there were ratings to consider. "From that lighting fixture."

The two cameramen both swung their cameras around and zoomed in for a close-up. Martin stifled a grin.

Johnny stepped into the center of the room and looked up. "Charles Pace, if you're here, we'd just like to talk to you, that's all. We're friendly and we'd like to listen to you. We know what happened to you, and you can tell us all about it."

Martin remembered the plan he'd made on the stairs, and he suddenly ran his hand over his face. "Is something on me? A bug or something?"

The cameras both swung his direction as David and Johnny examined him. "No, nothing," David said. "Did you feel something?"

"Yeah, I did…like…something light, brushing my face."

Johnny gestured at a digital camera set up in the corner of the room. "Let's see if we got anything else…" He pulled a walkie-talkie from his belt and thumbed the control, calling Marcus, the tech guy, out in the second van. "Marcus, you got anything in the upstairs bedroom?"

A voice crackled from the device's tinny speaker. "Not that I can see, but something might show up later on."

Martin stepped forward, letting the cameras linger on his sober expression as he said, "Guys, I think this house is very, very haunted."

He knew that would be a perfect commercial break.

The house was haunted. But it was not haunted by the dead spirits of those who had once dwelt there; rather, it was plagued by the living, who had exploited it and who now applied a label that it hadn't earned and didn't want. It only desired to rest or provide a home, not be the object of desperate and deluded men.

The house was no longer patient.

"So," Martin said, as he ran an EMF detector along the walls of the bedroom, "if the theory is that old houses act like recorders for everything that happens in them, and a suicide is a pretty big happening…then we should get something in this room."

"Oh, wait a minute…" That was David, scanning an opposite wall with his own gauge. "Yeah, I'm getting some spikes here." The cameramen descended on David, one punching in for a close-up on his EMF reading, the other pulling back for a wide shot.

Johnny joined him. "Wow, look at those readings! This is very serious evidence."

Martin half-smiled. "Hope Ms. Baker can find somebody who likes ghosts to buy this house."

No.

The house would no longer tolerate the presence of these caustic intruders. It wanted to feel the satisfaction of a job well done, to share in the contentedness of those living within it, and these men were jeopardizing its chances.

It fought back the only way it could.

Martin staggered and clutched at a wall for support.

His mind had suddenly filled with images that had come unbidden, but which he knew to be true: images of happier times, tableaux of bliss, pictures of comfort. He saw an old woman, who he knew was Millie Chautauqua, laugh as a grandchild rolled an old-fashioned ball to her. He saw Martha Joosten receive the gratitude of a friend who'd been helped by her teas. And he saw Charles Pace seated in a parlor room, his face alight with adoration as he gazed at a pretty young woman who batted her eyelashes at him.

He gasped as he realized these weren't his memories, but could only belong to the house itself.

"Hey, Martin, are you okay?" That was one of the cameramen, who had turned his lens on Martin.

"No. Wait…turn the cameras off."

The two cameramen looked at each uncertainly.

David stepped up and put a hand on Martin's shoulder, then spoke in low tones. "What's going on, bro? Are you in pain, or…?"

"Turn the goddamn cameras off!"

The two cameramen hesitated, then lowered their equipment.

Johnny joined his two companions. "What's going on?"

"This house…this fucking house…" The images had ceased unreeling in Martin's head, but the memories lingered—and they infuriated him. There'd been nothing there he could exploit. He couldn't sell a show on fucking pictures of grandmas playing ball, or suckers like Charlie Pace drooling in love. For the first time ever, he'd experienced an actual paranormal happening, and it was useless to him.

"What about the house?" David asked, perplexed.

"There's nothing here. We're wasting our time. We're not going to get anything here."

David and Johnny looked from each other to Martin. "But…you said something touched you…" Johnny said.

Martin shouted his response. "I always say that, you stupid kid. You say it, David says it…so fucking what?! We're not being touched by anything but the occasional spider or fleck of dust, and we all fucking know it."

Before anyone could respond, Martin tore off his *Ghostmasters* jacket, then reached for the plain white T-shirt he wore underneath, yanking it over his head.

David watched warily. "What are you doing?"

Martin dangled the shirt, which nearly glowed in the dim light, and stepped just out of the room. "I'm going to step out of the room where you can't see me, and then throw this across the doorway while you guys all video it."

Johnny frowned. "You mean…"

"Fucking right, Johnny. By the time they play it back, it's gonna look like the best goddamn ghost we've ever seen."

"We can't do that, Martin," said David, jaws tightening, "that would be…well, fraudulent. That's not what we're about."

"Oh, bullshit. We're about giving the rubes a little thrill at the same time every week. They need to believe in this shit to give their lives meaning, so they tune into us. See? Look at it that way and we're doing a good thing." Martin stepped out of the room and called from the hall, "We gonna do this?"

One of the cameramen shrugged and raised his camera. "I'm good." His coworker followed suit.

"Okay, here we go, on the count of three…one…two…three."

Martin tossed the shirt. It fluttered in the darkness and was gone.

"Got it," said one of the cameramen.

"You might want to punch it up a little in post, but it should work," said the other.

"I quit," Johnny said, as he started out of the room past Martin.

Martin called after him, "Fine. Then there'll be a lot of people hearing about how much coke you do to get through these night shoots."

Johnny hesitated, his shoulders drooped, and Martin knew he'd won.

"Now let's get the fuck out of this stupid fucking house."

Martin pulled his shirt and jacket back on, then led the way down the stairs and out the front door.

Eleanor Baker waited for them outside. "Well?"

"Oh, boy, Ms. Baker," Martin said with false enthusiasm, "you've got a severely fucked-up house on your hands here. Good luck with that sale." Then he turned and left the real estate woman gaping.

After the *Ghostmasters* vans had driven away, Eleanor turned and looked again at the house, which somehow always made her feel welcomed and warm, and she decided to see if the owners would accept her offer. She knew the house was worth more, but perhaps she could persuade them that it would be a tough sell once the *Ghostmasters* show aired.

She loved the house and wanted to take care of it.

The house had just experienced its worst memories ever. But it refused to let them imprint on its sensitive walls. It wouldn't force those scenes on anyone else, no matter how long it stood. It would leave those bad images for others to replay.

The house returned to slumber, and its dreams were good.

MONSTERS
of L.A.

CAT
PEOPLE

CAT PEOPLE

Nekomusume.

Amanda looked up from the strange word scrawled in her notepad and rolled the syllables around on her tongue, trying to imagine the correct pronunciation. She knew enough about Japanese to guess that one or more of the middle vowels might be essentially silent, but beyond that, she had no idea.

Jon would probably know just how to say it—or at least he would tell me how wrong I am, she thought, while making a small grimace. Somehow the grimace was as close as she got to a smile these days.

Nekomusume. Beside that word was another one, equally exotic: *yokai.*

She read over her notes again: "*Yokai* = supernatural spirits in Japanese mythology. *Nekomusume* = a *yokai* that's a catwoman. *La Japonesa = nekomusume.*"

Amanda took another sip of her flavored iced tea and looked up, scanning the street from where she sat on a concrete bench under the awning of a cheap taco stand in the bowels of the San Gabriel Valley. The only other customer was seated two tables away, a fat man of indeterminate ethnicity, tucking into a greasy taco as if it was his last meal.

In this area, it could well be.

She shifted on the hard plastic bench, wishing she were somewhere else. It was hot and smoggy, and she didn't belong here, on the other end of L.A. from her safe university enclave. Her blouse was sticking to her skin, and she was suddenly aware of how far away she'd parked. She should have been back in an air-conditioned classroom, telling a bunch of disinterested college kids that there was more to American folklore than Paul Bunyan and his blue ox.

At least she didn't have to come home to Jon. Her quiet, empty guesthouse, tucked away in a canyon above the campus, was better than the expensive three-bedroom estate full of the noise of failure.

It was now a quarter after three, and she was starting to think she'd been the victim of a joke. The two kids who'd claimed to have seen Southern California's *La Japonesa* (and who'd agreed to meet her here at three) hadn't showed, and Amanda could imagine them right now, hanging with their friends, laughing about the lady professor they'd punked.

But that didn't explain why they'd given an interview to the local newspaper, the *El Monte Tribune*.

Amanda looked up and noticed the fat man had finished his taco and was staring at her, with something halfway between open hostility and sardonic amusement. She felt a gush of adrenaline, pure fight-or-flight instinct, and decided to leave.

Provided she could.

She was just closing up her notebook when the throb of a deep engine announced a fresh arrival in the taco stand's lot. The car was a new SUV, black, an expensive model, and Amanda wondered who could afford a car like that in this rundown area of Southern California. Jon had gotten their SUV in the divorce settlement; on her salary, she could barely afford a six-year-old sedan.

The doors opened and two Latino kids got out. They were dressed in the uniform of their generation—baggy jeans, designer sneakers, sports team jerseys—and they nodded as they saw her.

"Hey, you Miz Houston?" said the taller boy.

Amanda nodded and relaxed slightly. "Yes. You must be Tommy and Rafael."

"That's us."

Amanda was gratified to see that the fat man had given up watching her and slunk off.

The two kids ordered drinks, then joined her at the table. "So you wanna know about *La Japonesa*, huh?" Rafael asked her. He was smaller than Tommy, with an acne-scarred face and at least three rings on each hand.

"Yes, among other things."

Tommy squinted at her. "What other things?"

"I'm writing a book called *Folklore in Transition*. There's a lot of local stuff in it."

Rafael said, "You mean more weird shit like the cat-lady?"

Amanda nodded. "Right. But let's talk about what you saw." Then, hoping she'd copied their accents, she added, "*La Japonesa.*"

Their grins vanished, and in that instant Amanda believed they'd seen *something*.

Tommy hunched forward, narrowing his bulky shoulders. "It was pretty fuckin' creepy—oh, sorry."

"That's okay," Amanda said. She flipped the notebook open again and got a pen ready. "Had you heard of *La Japonesa* before?"

The boys exchanged a quick glance, and Rafael played with his rings. "Sure. Everybody's heard of her—the cat-lady up in the hills. Sometimes she takes out a dog or somethin'. Last year when that hiker was mauled, they said it was a mountain lion, but we know it was her. *La Japonesa.*"

Check hiker story, Amanda noted, then asked, "What else had you heard?"

Rafael answered. "My *tia* told me that she was, like, this spirit brought over from Japan by these Spanish traders; and she was really pissed off at being brought here, like two hundred years ago; so she took this form of a cat-lady and killed people every once in a while."

"Did you know other people who'd seen her?"

Another quick look, then Tommy said, "No."

"So tell me about what happened when you saw her."

Rafael leaned forward, excited. "It was two weeks ago. Real hot night, and me and Tommy, we couldn't sleep; so we decided to go up into the hills—"

Amanda cut in, "At night?"

The two boys looked mildly nervous, and when Tommy answered, Amanda thought he was lying. "Yeah, we…uh…go up there sometimes to…y'know…smoke a little."

Amanda nodded, trying to look as if she believed them. "So this one night…"

"Yeah," Rafael went on, "we're up there and it's about three in the morning, and we hear something just below us, and then we see these eyes, you know, shining. Like a cat's eyes, yellow with slit pupils, but big, and we're like, Ah, shit, it's a mountain lion! But then we get our flashlight pointed at it, and there's a human face around the eyes—"

Tommy added, " — and it's a woman, and she's beautiful, but she's got these big ears that stick up, like a cat's, and it looks like she's even got more than one tail — "

Amanda jotted down some notes, then said, "What happened next?"

"She fuckin' growled at us," Rafael said, and Amanda thought the glint of fear in his expression was probably real. "And we ran. I mean, we just took off, figurin' the whole way that this thing would catch us and tear us up any second; but… it didn't."

Tommy twisted the straw in his drink. "But the next morning they found a dead dog up there, torn apart. And I'm thinkin' that fuckin' dog saved our lives, man — she went after it instead of us. Otherwise we might not be here talkin' to you."

Amanda made a last note (*dog mauled?*) and asked, "Do you think you could take me to where you saw her?"

The look of dismay and — what, deceit? — that passed between the two boys was obvious. "No, we can't do that," said Tommy.

"Why not?"

"Because…we're afraid to go up there now."

Rafael said, "Besides, we were…uh…stoned that night. We couldn't really find it again anyway."

Amanda finished writing, then closed her notebook and looked up at them. "Okay, I think that's it. Thanks for your time. Feel free to e-mail or call me if you think of anything else."

"Oh, there is one other thing…" Tommy added.

Amanda paused halfway off the bench and waited.

The two boys exchanged a look, then Rafael snorted and turned away, leaving Tommy to go on nervously, "I…since that night, I've been…dreaming about her. Like, these dreams feel real, like she's there all the time now."

Amanda stared at him for a beat, not knowing how to respond.

"So are we, like, gonna be in your book?" asked Rafael.

That broke Amanda's paralysis, and she turned away. "I'll let you know."

She left without looking back.

"They were lying."

"I'm not so sure."

Sam paused, forkful of salad halfway to his mouth. "C'mon, Mandy—they're publicity hounds."

Amanda sipped her tea and glanced around the crowded university cafeteria. "Maybe, but I think they really saw something up there."

Her friend set down his fork and looked her straight in the eye. Sam West was older than Amanda, with unashamed gray in his beard and an air of confidence; he had long ago achieved the tenure she was still struggling for. "I know how important this book is to you, and yes—you need to publish, it'll boost your shot at tenure, it'll help you recover from the divorce, all of that…but don't tell me you actually believe any of this."

"No, but I'd like to." Amanda pushed her cup aside, warming to the subject. "You remember the story, right?"

Sam made a wry face. "Of course."

Of course—it'd been a stupid question. Sam's book *Crying Women and Cat Spirits: Mexican Folklore North of the Border* had inspired Amanda's interest in *La Japonesa*.

"Okay, I know you do, but just hear me out: So the story starts in Mexico, as a traditional folktale about a legendary cat-woman who's brought over from Japan by Spanish traders in the 17th century, right? Her spirit is trapped in an urn that they carelessly leave beside a cactus patch. She finally escapes the urn and becomes a vengeful monster, a cat with four tails that kills anyone who comes near the urn. At some point the immigrants come north over the border to America and bring the story with them, and now *La Japonesa* is still haunting the Southern California hills four centuries later, so—Sam, I think this is the best example in California of a traditional folktale that's still alive, still evolving."

Sam nodded, considering. "I can see that."

Amanda continued, "I checked the news of the mauled hiker that those kids mentioned, and it was real—they never did catch whatever killed that hiker. And all the eyewitness reports say she's beautiful…"

Sam laughed. "Yeah, okay—I'd like an eyeful of her, too."

"And she's the perfect symbol of Southern California folklore—a blend of different cultures. A mix of ghost, human, and animal. The ultimate icon of the Los Angeles melting pot."

Sam chewed for a second, then said, "Just reassure me of one thing: that this isn't some midlife crisis thing, where the woman hurt in the messy divorce fixates on a strong female figure."

Amanda laughed. But she didn't really smile.

The next day, Amanda took a hike into the foothills above El Monte.

She wore jeans, a sweatshirt, and heavy hiking boots, and she tucked her styled and dyed hair up under a baseball cap that Jon had left behind. She started up a trail about four in the afternoon, moving from sage and cactus, gravel and dust, up to manzanita, scrub pine, and boulder. Although she saw small clusters of trash that might have been either stoners' hangouts or homeless camps, she encountered no one else. At one point she found a sturdy six-foot length of tree limb and turned it into a walking staff, although its heft in her hands made her feel safer for other reasons.

She knew it was unwise to stay in the hills after dark (she wouldn't have wanted to encounter Tommy and Rafael up here, she thought with some irony) that there was no point to it… but all of the witnesses to *La Japonesa* had reported sighting her between the hours of two and four a.m., and Amanda thought she knew why:

In Japanese mythology, that period (which was a single hour in the old Japanese method of reckoning time) was called "the hour of the ox." It was a time when *yokai* were traditionally easiest to see. *Yokai* like *La Japonesa*.

So she found a shelter made by a large boulder to the back and a patch of grassy earth beneath it, spread a blanket, and sat down to wait.

The first hour after sunset was unnerving, and Amanda jumped at every skitter and bird cry. As night deepened, she found herself strangely soothed by the panorama of the L.A. cityscape lit up below her. The evening was warm, the air clearer at even this slight altitude; and Amanda found a contemplative space she hadn't known in some time.

She thought about her book; she'd been working on it for over a year and had hundreds of pages of notes, but little finished text. She contemplated her classes. Her friends. Her failed marriage.

And she didn't much like what she saw.

She was in the middle of a life that hadn't been extraordinary. She was nearly forty and had realized no dreams. Achieved no serious goals. Had little to show. The day Jon had told her he was leaving, he'd called her "a serious underachiever."

She thought he was probably right.

The lights below were redolent of a glittering history that Amanda had never really claimed; she'd tried to embrace the stories and adventures, but they'd always felt too far outside of her mundane reality. She wanted to be special, part of something bigger than herself…but neither marriage nor academic life had provided solace. She shivered, and realized that even this expedition had been reduced to practical considerations—would she be able to find her way back in the dark? Did she have anything she could use for warmth…or a weapon? When she finally checked the time on her cell phone, she was surprised to see it was after three in the morning.

The Hour of the Ox.

Just as she lowered the cell phone, she heard it: a low, guttural snarl somewhere off in the dark.

Amanda froze, all thoughts of Jon and failings abruptly shut down.

A small cascade of gravel, somewhere off to her right. Maybe a hundred feet.

Amanda drew herself up against the boulder, grabbed at the large stick she'd acquired, holding it out before her. She jumped as more skittering pebbles sounded. Whatever was out there, it was circling her.

Getting closer.

Should see turn on the flashlight, see if she could spot it? Or would that just make her an easier target?

Another growl, this time to her left. It had gone around her, 180 degrees. It could obviously already see, or scent her. The flashlight probably wouldn't make much difference.

She turned it on, pointing it towards the location of the last noise.

The beam fell on glowing cat eyes.

At first Amanda felt a thrill, exhilaration. Then she saw the face around the eyes—the tawny pelt, large wet nose, long teeth.

A mountain lion.

Amanda cried out, and involuntarily swung the branch in a semicircle. The huge cat snarled, turned and fled.

Amanda sat huddled against the rock, panting, her heart thundering; she felt pain in her left hand and realized she'd scraped her skin against the rock and was bleeding. She was sure the predator would smell her blood, hear her terror and return, that the last thing she'd feel would be its hot breath in her face as its claws caused her flesh to sing in agony.

The flashlight shook in her hands, the beam jittery as it raked the high desert landscape around her. After fifteen minutes the light died, and Amanda shoved it back in her knapsack. She had some matches with her, and she used them to make a fire from some nearby twigs. She knew it was fire season and that her actions were dangerous, but she made a ring in the dirt around her small blaze and felt safer.

When the sun finally came up, Amanda stumbled down the hillside. She reached her car, staggered in, locked the doors, and then let herself shake for a few moments.

When all that was left was emptiness, she started up the car and drove home.

Two days later, Sam showed her a story in the paper about two kids in El Monte who'd been caught growing marijuana at a location hidden in the hills. They'd had roughly 2,000 plants up there, plants they'd grown with water hijacked from a city water reserve.

The boys were identified as Rafael Gomez, 18, and Tomas Mendoza, 19.

"Looks like they made up the *La Japonesa* story to scare off people from going up there and finding their little rancho. Didn't work, I guess," Sam said.

"No, I guess it didn't," Amanda answered.

"How's the book coming?"

"Oh…well, I can finish out the chapter on the cat-woman now."

Sam smiled. "Yeah. Are you going to title it '*La Japonesa*, Guardian of Pot Farms'?"

Amanda hadn't told Sam (or anyone else) about her little overnight stay in the hills, so she knew he wouldn't understand if she told him that her own private joke title for that chapter was "*La Japonesa*, Mountain Lyin'."

And the subtitle would have been, "The Night I Lost the Last of My Hope."

A week later, Amanda received an e-mail from Tommy: "You probly know we got busted. But we didnt lie about

La Japonesa—we really saw her. And Im still having dreams."

Then Amanda read the last line of the e-mail, and felt a tremor race along her spine:

"And she knows about you."

Amanda's job would be up for review in a month.

Enrollment in the university's folklore studies program was down, even with the minor celebrity status of Sam West, who'd once hit a local bestseller list with one of his books. Amanda knew she needed to show something—a manuscript, at least, even if there was no publishing deal yet.

She tried to work seriously on *Folklore in Transition*. She started collating her notes, trying to lose herself in stories of the supposed curse on Griffith Park. Of the Roosevelt Hotel in Hollywood, haunted by the ghosts of celebrities. Of animals predicting earthquakes, and Mexican *botanicas* that cured with herbs and spirits, and the 1930s prospector G. Warren Shufelt and his search for the serpent people's tunnels of gold beneath the city.

But mostly she came back to *La Japonesa*. What had once been a symbol of the way L.A. melded varying cultures had now become emblematic of the city's ability to shatter illusion.

Summer was running late this year—it was mid-October, and the nighttime temperatures were still in the 80s. Amanda's guesthouse, nestled against a canyon wall, sheltered by a chaotic mix of hibiscus and palm, stayed cooler than the house she'd shared with Jon had, but it was still warm enough at night that she left the windows open while she worked.

She was pulling late-nighters recently, a lot of them spent

staring at a laptop screen and a bewildering mess of hundreds of pages of scribbled notes. Tonight she'd actually managed to type a few paragraphs, but now it was after 2 a.m., and she felt her attention span slipping away.

She was about to turn off the laptop when a phrase caught her eye: *The Hour of the Ox.*

It was after 2 a.m. now. *Synchronicity in action,* she thought. *Jung would be proud.*

She turned away—and gasped as she saw something glittering in the darkness just outside her open windows: a pair of yellow eyes, with cat pupils.

Jesus, a mountain lion here?

She froze, staring hard into the darkness, trying to think of something she could use as a weapon, or as protection—

The eyes moved then, towards the window, until they were just before the screen; and that was when Amanda saw the human nose and mouth.

La Japonesa looked in at her.

Amanda was terrified. This wasn't revelation, or transcendence, but pure, heart-pounding fear. The hair on the back of her neck prickled, and her fingers curled into fists.

She wanted to yell at the thing, to send it away, but she could utter no sounds beyond a slight croak.

It found me, she thought, and then remembered that night on the hill, a scraped palm: *because of my blood.*

The creature at the window lifted a limb. It was the length and structure of a human arm, but was covered in a short, silky golden fur and had claws on the ends of the fingers, claws that unsheathed as Amanda watched. The cat-woman gently drew the claws across the surface of the screen, and the mesh parted like a lover's lips.

She pulled the screen apart—and then leapt up to the sill and over, into the room.

Amanda didn't move. She watched paralyzed, knowing that even if she could get up and run she'd never outrace this thing. It stood on two powerful, lightly furred back legs, and had four long, thin tails.

Four. In Japanese, the word for "four"—*shi*—sounded like the word for "death."

But if *La Japonesa* intended to murder Amanda, it wouldn't happen quickly. Instead the catwoman peered at Amanda for a long moment, her almond-shaped, wine-colored eyes expressing great interest, even affection.

She knows, thought Amanda. *It's impossible, but…she knows I'm writing about her.*

La Japonesa moved towards her.

Amanda smelled a powerful animal musk and drew back, although there was nowhere to go. The catwoman seemed to sense Amanda's fear, and her face (the small part of Amanda that could still articulate thought, *My God, she is exquisite*) subtly shifted, her lovely pink mouth drawing slowly up.

She took another step, and another, until she stood a few feet away, and then she slowly raised one hand/paw, a single claw extended. Amanda flinched as the paw approached her face, but she couldn't stop watching as the downy-pelted fingers reached for her forehead, gently slid down her face—

—and then she felt the pain as the claw pierced her cheek.

She cried out and did close her eyes now, not wanting to see where the claw went next, expecting to feel the pain, her flesh being torn open, the smell of her blood and its heat as it spilled from her, her death happening as she felt every nerve twitch and pulse…

But it didn't happen.

She finally opened her eyes again, just in time to see *La Japonesa* jump to the sill, turning back to look at Amanda a last time before she vanished into the night.

Amanda was shaking badly; her legs felt bloodless, but she managed to get up, slam all the windows shut and check the locks, then stagger into the bathroom. The cut on her right cheek was no more than two inches long, but it was deep, and Amanda knew it would leave a permanent scar.

She'd been marked.

As she watched a gauze pad held up to the wound redden, she knew she'd see that scar for the rest of her life, every morning when she looked into a mirror. Students, friends, and lovers alike would see it, and ask how she'd gotten it. Most she'd lie to, tell them she'd been careless with a cat.

A few she'd answer truthfully.

She thought she'd never see *La Japonesa* again, or anything else like her, but whenever she saw that narrow white ridge on her face, she would know, know that she'd been allowed into the mysteries, that she was now a part of something vast and old, and untamed.

Amanda smiled.

MONSTERS of L.A.

THE
CREATURE

THE CREATURE

Billy Danning pointed at the tar pit and exclaimed, "Look, Mommy — it's bubbling."

Billy's mother, Ashley, barely looked up from her phone conversation. "…oh, I know, can you believe it?" she continued, trying to wave her eight-year-old son to silence, "he's such a douchebag. I mean, the first one was bad enough…"

It was a crowded, sunny Sunday around the La Brea Tar Pits: couples posed for photos with the giant sloth statue, kids ran shrieking along the concrete walkways that bordered the glassy black pits, parents chattered on cell phones or punched in text messages. Yet, despite the substantial crowd, only Billy was watching the bubble forming in the tar, plainly visible just beyond the fence and a short grassy expanse; a few feet to the side of the bubbling, a huge plaster mastodon was eternally sucked to its doom as its family watched from the safety of the bank.

The bubble expanded to nearly two feet across, popped loudly, and promptly grew again.

"Mom…" Billy said, now tugging his mother's sleeve and gesturing with more urgency.

"Billy, stop it." Ashley glared at him briefly, then shrugged off his grubby fingers and went back to her call. "Sorry; we're at the La Brea Tar Pits and Billy's getting all excited by *tar*…oh, I know it's incredibly dumb, but we drove past here last week on the way to a play date, and he saw those retarded elephant statues or whatever they are, and he simply *had* to come here today."

Ashley turned and walked a few feet off. Billy looked back at the oily surface—

—and something broke it.

At first it was so ooze-covered that it was hard to make out the shape pushing its way slowly up out of the liquid asphalt, but as Billy watched, paralyzed, sludge fell away and revealed a large hand with webbed, clawed fingers.

"He doesn't give a shit about his own son," Ashley was saying behind him. "Ever since he took up with that slut, Billy doesn't even exist."

The hand became an arm, reaching up. The arm was connected to a shoulder…then the top of a head pushed through the surface…one inch, two, three, four, and Billy knew that head plainly belonged to something that wasn't human.

"MOMMY!" he screamed.

Ashley whirled. "For God's sake, Billy, what—?!" Then she followed his madly waving hand, and saw the creature that was agonizingly, impossibly emerging from the tar, using a leg of the fake mastodon to haul itself up.

"Holy shit," she said, then remembered the cell phone. "Angie, can I call you right back? Yeah. Okay. Bye."

She finished the call and turned her attention fully to the creature. A crowd was gathering now, a murmur growing. Billy danced excitedly, nearly hyperventilating.

"It's a monster; it's a monster—!"

Ashley laughed. "Don't be ridiculous, honey. It's a guy in a suit. It's probably a promotion for a new movie or something."

The crowd picked up on Ashley's statement, and guesses began to percolate. "Aren't they doing a new swamp monster movie?" said a tall man with glasses. "I think I saw a commercial for this," said a woman, as she fiddled with the camera settings on her smart phone. "That's pretty fucking cool," said a kid with three lip piercings.

"Billy, do you remember how to work the video camera on Mommy's phone?" Ashley asked.

The creature now had one leg on land and was awkwardly trying to pull itself free from the last of the tar's embrace, grasping onto an imitation mastodon tusk. As more tar and water sluiced off it, a scaled, faintly greenish hide was revealed, and trembling flaps on either side of its face that looked like gills. It had no nose, no hair, and huge amphibious eyes.

Somehow, Billy instinctively knew it wanted to kill him. He reached for Ashley's hand and tried to pull her away. "Mom, we have to GO—!"

Ashley ignored him, stabbing triumphantly at the screen on her phone. "There's the video!" She lifted the phone and pointed it at the creature, who had planted both clawed feet on land.

The excitement in the onlookers grew. Cameras and phones were held aloft. "My followers are going to fucking love this," blurted out a young man wearing a T-shirt featuring a horror movie poster. A giggling teenaged girl turned to her friend and said, "Maybe this is a reality show and we'll be on MTV."

Ashley lowered the phone and hit a number, then raised the phone to her lips again. "Ange, you've gotta see this—check out the picture I just sent you. They're doing some kind of crazy promotion here today…yeah, that guy in the photo just came up out of the tar…no, you can't even see his oxygen tanks or whatever. Isn't that awesome?"

The creature shambled up past the statuary to the fence, leaving a trail of tar behind it. It reached out to the bars, beat its hands against the barrier once—then it grasped the fence and simply tore a section aside, the snapping metal sounding like machine-gun pops.

The audience applauded.

"Dude, that rocked!" "What movie is this for?" "I hope we get free T-shirts!" "I didn't even notice that section of fence was fake…"

But Billy wasn't clapping or waiting to be handed a promotional baseball cap—he was screaming. So were a few others, but not many.

"God, Billy, shut UP!" Ashley said, then returned to her call. "I swear, he is such a little geek sometimes…"

Overcome by animal panic, Billy ran. He skirted around the crowd and dodged a few others who were likewise fleeing. He sped past a figure of a giant prehistoric bear, but when he found his path blocked by more gawkers, he leapt into a tree, scrambling into the branches until he was eight feet overhead. He crouched on a limb there, shaking violently, bobbing his head until he could see what was happening.

The creature, freed now from the encumbrance of its tar prison, was picking up speed. It abruptly lunged and grabbed one of the giggling teenaged girls, who shrieked with glee.

Then it tore her neck open.

Billy burst into tears. A few of the audience screamed and ran—but most held their ground, laughing, clapping, pointing, taking photos, texting. Blood gushed from the girl's neck, mixing with tar as the creature tossed her back into its oily path. "What a stunt!" Billy heard someone yell.

He saw his mom then. Ashley was still talking on her phone, taking pictures, sending photos. She was grinning when the creature reached out and tore its claws across her face, taking one ear, one eye, most of one cheekbone and a large patch of scalp.

Billy howled. He had one last glimpse of his mother's look of shock, before she crumpled and was lost from sight.

The creature rampaged through the park, killing six and wounding four others before the crowds vanished and were replaced by police, who chased it into the Page Museum. Later on, the papers claimed that the thing was killed by a barrage of gunfire (that also destroyed a complete fossil Dire Wolf skeleton and most of the diorama on the wall behind it); but no one saw the body, and not long after there were rumors of secret government experiments being conducted on the still-living creature, at Edwards Air Force Base, just north of L.A.

Billy Danning spent two weeks with his father, but Steven Danning had recently remarried and was so preoccupied with playing father to his two new stepdaughters that he had no time for Billy (who Steven's new wife despised). Billy was shunted off to his maternal grandparents, who inexplicably blamed Ashley's death on the boy; Billy was fed, clothed, and housed, but given little else. He grew up as a quiet, sullen boy who barely passed his school courses and was deemed a problem child by counselors and teachers.

When Billy was 15, the zombie apocalypse happened. During the first, devastating wave, Billy's grandparents nailed boards over windows, moved in darkness, and whispered to each other, trying to draw no attention. One night as they slept, Billy loosened the boards, ran into the backyard with a ladder, climbed up onto the roof, pulled the ladder up after him, and then — as dawn broke — blew repeatedly into a vuvuzela until he was delirious from lack of oxygen. The living dead quickly surrounded the house and easily broke through the sabotaged boards, and on the roof, Billy grinned from ear to ear as he listened to the shrieks of his grandparents while they were being devoured.

Unfortunately, Billy's plan had failed to consider his own escape, and after several weeks on the roof he died of starvation and exposure. The last thing he saw before his eyes rolled up in his head, were the reanimated corpses of his grandparents and his mother, all staring up at him with more interest than any of them had ever shown him when they'd actually been alive.

MONSTERS
of L.A.

THE
ALIEN

THE ALIEN

"What is *that* thing?"

Donna Morrison turned to see what her husband Howard was talking about, and together they looked down at the blue and purple plant sprouting from the sandy California soil. The shrub—or succulent, or small tree, or whatever it was—had blade-like leaves radiating out from a central pod and a single, segmented trunk sprouting up several feet into the air, ending in a puffy green ball.

"Well," Donna said, "that is unusual."

Howard moved further along the paved walk, scanning the ground. "This one doesn't have a little plaque telling you what it is."

Glancing around, Donna saw that, indeed, it seemed to be the only specimen in this area of the arboretum without a printed name. "It must be new—so new they haven't made up the sign yet."

Howard grunted, then said, "You're right about it being new. I don't remember seeing it when we were here for the last sale."

Donna raised her bottle of imported water and glanced up into the sky. The weather today was classic gorgeous Southern

California—hot (especially for February) smogless and clear, a slight, dry breeze gently toying with the foliage that surrounded them. Donna cherished the county arboretum, with its wide-open central expanse and little clusters of different plant types in every nook; she guessed that Howard, though, came only to the occasional sales to buy something for their yard that would make the neighbors gape in envy. Status was very important to Howard.

"I wonder," Howard said, looking back towards the exhibit hall that housed the exotic plants for sale today, "if they have one of these?"

"We wouldn't know what to do with it." Donna bent to take a closer look. "Those leaves almost look dangerous."

"Don't be ridiculous, Donna. They wouldn't put a dangerous plant right out here in the open, in a public park."

"I guess, but…" Something about the plant unnerved Donna, and she jumped when one of the roaming arboretum peacocks screamed from a few yards away. She hadn't seen it perched on the lower branches of a nearby oak, its glorious plumage spread, its black eye cast upon her.

"Why is it staring at us?"

Howard's head jerked up. "What?"

"Nothing." Donna turned to walk away. "Let's go look at the water gardens."

"Hold on…" Howard was pulling his smart phone out and positioning it above the plant. "I want a picture of this."

He snapped several shots, examined them critically on the tiny screen, and grunted again. "Colors look different in a picture."

The plant was somehow making Donna increasingly anxious, and she once again turned to move away. "It's getting late…"

"It's only two. Let's see if we can find someone who knows about this."

Howard looked around, scanning the arboretum grounds, trying to find an employee. He started to trounce off toward the cluster of administrative buildings near the front entrance, but stopped when he realized Donna wasn't with him. "Donna—"

Something was happening to Donna. Suddenly she didn't want to leave the plant; it was as if it was a star, a sun, a center of gravity, and she was a satellite, clinging to its influence. She felt her control slipping away, but her anxiety was going with it, and she didn't panic; instead, she liked the feeling of looseness, of something opening within her.

Howard peered at her uncertainly. "Donna, are you—?"

She cut him off. "I'm fine, Howard. Despite the fact that twenty years of marriage to you have killed all my dreams and hopes." Her voice was even and lilting, but her eyes were unfocused.

Howard stared for a second in silent, absolute shock, then stuttered out, "What do you—I haven't—"

Donna continued, ignoring him. "Our lives are meaningless, Howard. We have an expensive house, a yard full of exotic plants that are taken care of by someone else, and two grown children who barely ever talk to us."

This time Howard actually staggered back a step. "Donna, what…are you having sunstroke?"

She blinked, and her pupils suddenly contracted to the proper size again. Staggering slightly, Donna put a hand to her head. "I'm sorry, were…were you saying something?"

"No, but you were."

"I was?"

Donna searched her immediate memory, but there were no words, only images—the strange plant, the turquoise sky, the nearby hills, Howard…the plant.

"I think I need to take you home." Howard reached for his wife, but she pulled away in annoyance.

"Stop. I'm fine. Really."

He was about to argue when a park employee walked past them. Howard and Donna, with the insecure discretion of the privileged American, abruptly shut up and froze, waiting…but the dark-skinned man in the white polo shirt, name badge, and khakis stopped and knelt by the plant. As they watched, he inserted some sort of instrument into the dirt around the plant and brushed its leaves with loving care.

Donna nodded down at the man and spoke softly to her husband. "Weren't you going to try to find an employee?"

"I was, but…"

"What? Go ahead. Ask him about the plant."

Howard looked down at the man and saw that his skin was an indefinable shade of dark olive; it was a hue Howard had never seen on a human being. The employee's hair was black and glossy, his limbs and features moderately proportioned and handsome…but somehow his very *foreign-ness* disturbed and irritated Howard.

"I doubt if he speaks English."

"Well, if he works here, he must."

"Why? Our gardener at home doesn't speak English."

Donna sighed. "God, Howard, of *course* Armando speaks English. I talk to him every week when he comes."

Howard's eyebrows rose. "You do? What do you talk about, 'when he comes'?"

"His duties, mainly."

"Like what?"

Donna felt that other influence exerting itself again, and she let it. "Okay, Howard, you got me: Armando fucks me every Wednesday afternoon at exactly 3:15 p.m., while you're at work and I'm home pretending to be something more than just another one of your possessions."

"Jesus Christ, Donna—" He was starting to raise his voice, but was suddenly aware of the brown-skinned man crouching nearby. "Look, I'm leaving. You can go or stay; I don't really give a shit which."

She eyed the employee with overt interest. "Good. I think I'll stay."

Howard felt his adrenaline spike; he wanted to beat something, anything. "Fine. You stay here, then, with one more illegal who probably doesn't have papers and should be deported before he gets his next assignment from Al Qaeda."

"You're hateful, Howard. I'm going to prove you're wrong."

With that, Donna strode up to the employee boldly and bent down near him. "Excuse me…"

He looked up, his teeth gleaming and white; his voice was light and mellow, only a slight trace of accent. "Hello. May I help you?"

Donna shot Howard a quick, boastful smile, then returned her attention to the man. "We were wondering about this plant. We come to the arboretum a few times a year, but we've never seen it before."

The employee rose. His name badge read FZYGR, T. Donna wondered if it was a typo.

"Oh, yes, this just came to us last week." He gestured grandly at the plant. "It's a really unusual variety, isn't it? Note the variegated coloring and the spore production organ at the top of the central trunk..."

Howard snarled, "Yeah, yeah, but what the hell is it?"

Mr. Fzygr smiled and said, "We don't really know."

"What do you mean, you 'don't really know'? Of course you know. They wouldn't allow it to be put here if they didn't know what it was."

The gardener's warm expression didn't falter. "Oh, well, you see, sir—we didn't put it here. It simply appeared."

Howard looked down at the plant and realized now that its gleaming blue and purple base leaves almost looked metallic. "Then...but it could be dangerous."

"Oh, it's not dangerous...is it?"

The man looked past Howard's shoulder. Howard spun and saw three more of the park employees surrounding them now. They all had different shades of dark skin and distinct features, but they all wore the same placid, mild smile. "It's quite safe," said the one nearest to Howard.

Howard instinctively moved to his wife's side and put a protective arm about her waist. "Ah, well, I'm sure it is, but we're late for a lunch, so we'll—"

Donna twisted free of his grasp. "We'll do what, Howard? Run away before the filthy foreigners club us for our money? You're disgusting." She turned away from him back to the plant.

The grins of the employees all broadened.

"Look," Howard said, starting to backpedal, "whatever's going on here...I'm gone. Donna, you do whatever you want; but I'm getting out of here now."

He'd only taken three steps, however, before Mr. Fzygr's pleasant voice called out after him, "Oh, Sir..."

Against his better judgment, Howard stopped and looked back. The gardener was using a pair of shears to snip away one of the heavy leaves, and as he rose he extended it to Howard. "I'm sorry for any misunderstanding. Please take this cutting as a gift."

Howard just stared, but Donna gasped and reached out. "Oh, that's fantastic—"

"Donna, don't touch it—!"

Too late—his wife's fingers closed around the cutting. A shiver, an almost sexual trembling, coursed through her; then she walked up to Howard and held out the offering. "Oh, this will look so lovely in our yard, won't it?"

Something irresistible pushed up against Howard's consciousness. He struggled against it for a microsecond, but it was a superior force, and his resistance melted away. Gratefully, he reached out to accept the leaf. "Is there anything we should know about taking care of it?"

The first employee spoke again. "It's really very hardy and easy to care for, and it will reach maturity quickly. In fact, you'll probably be able to share cuttings from your plant in just a few weeks."

"Thank you." Howard walked towards the arboretum exit, and this time Donna went with him.

As they passed through the old-fashioned revolving door, Howard said, "I think I'll quit my job. I hate it, you know."

"I know," Donna said, as they walked toward the parking lot, and she reached out her fingers to stroke the cutting in Howard's hands.

"Oh," Howard added as an afterthought, "and I'm going to buy a gun and shove it right up that fucking Armando's ass."

MONSTERS
of L.A.

KAIJU
(GIANT MONSTER)

KAIJU

As the giant monster lifted its mansion-sized head from the waters of the Santa Monica Bay, Nick Stadtlinger was still hitting on the two bored Valley girls at the sunglasses stand on the boardwalk. Nick was just telling them that he'd once taken second place in a local surfing competition (not entirely a lie—he'd won the runner-up prize of a $25 gift certificate to Tacos Muchachos in a raffle sponsored by a Redondo Beach surf shop). The girls were plainly more interested in trying on sunglasses ("Oh, I'm like, I dunno, they're kind of stupid") than they were in trying on Nick.

Then Nick and the girls, and all the other thousands of sunbathers, swimmers, hustlers, and tourists, saw the thing rising up out of the bay, interrupting the usual routine of a clear, warm day at the beach; and for a frozen few seconds all talking ceased.

The monster—covered in the filthy black sludge from the bottom of the bay, so its real colors and form couldn't be made out—belted out a roar that violated eardrums and vibrated in chests.

Nick Stadtlinger knew his golden moment had come.

All 32 years of his life, Nick had really wanted only one thing: to be famous. He didn't care about being rich, or talented, or good-looking; he figured that the first would come with fame, the second didn't matter anyway, and he already possessed the third. His quest for fame had taken him from acting (why did he have to remember all those ridiculous lines when he could simply make up his own?) to music (since his parents refused to buy him a very expensive instrument, he would clearly never be truly proficient) to sports (that would have required cutting back on his beer, and *that* was simply not going to happen). He briefly considered a life of crime, but he really wasn't a bad person, and anyway, he wanted to be famous, not *infamous*.

He knew he was destined to be a hero.

The problem with being a hero was that it required waiting for the opportunities to present themselves. He couldn't, after all, throw a toddler in the path of a speeding truck and then rescue the child, or set fire to a nursing home and then bravely spirit the aged inhabitants to safety. No, he'd have to wait. Unfortunately, his life (living with his parents in Downey, home of The Carpenters, and working in his uncle's hardware store) had thus far failed to provide Nick with any real imminent catastrophes.

Until today.

By the time Nick realized *this is it*, the monster was about to set foot on the shore. Swimsuit-clad revelers were screaming and fleeing in droves past Nick; even the pair of Valley girls had already fled. Nick saw the monster's ooze-coated front foot lift out of the water and descend onto sand, and he started waving his arms, pointing and shouting.

"That way, everybody! That way!"

No one paid the slightest attention to Nick, of course. This wasn't going to work.

He remembered that the Pacific Coast Highway was a short distance behind him, and traffic was always thick there. He turned and ran, hearing the giant *thuds* of the monster's footfalls approaching. He glanced back once, but saw that the monster was moving very slowly; in fact, it seemed to be stepping carefully, as if trying to avoid causing injury or harm.

In a few minutes, Nick reached the edge of the PCH and saw the usual amount of cars speeding along, apparently blissfully unaware of the approaching horror. Nick leaped into the southbound lanes, waving his arms and screaming for the drivers to turn back.

A car approaching Nick at seventy miles per hour swerved to avoid him and collided with a car in the adjoining lane. Nick ducked as metal and glass from the wreck flew around him, while the two cars rolled and skidded, and finally came to a halt.

One of the drivers climbed out of his steaming, smashed machine, looked around, spotted Nick, and shrieked at him. Before he could approach, however, the monster came into view, towering over the lip of the highway, bellowing again.

Nick knew then that his work wasn't done. He jogged across the rest of the PCH, past Ocean Avenue and up onto Wilshire Boulevard. Pedestrians had already spotted the lumbering horror and were racing helter-skelter. Nick looked around, desperately hoping to spot an elderly woman needing help or a mother with a baby, but all he saw were businesspeople and shoppers.

He ran to the Third Street Promenade, then risked a look back. The monster was stepping across the PCH, still moving cautiously, miraculously avoiding cars, people, and structures. But it was definitely coming this way.

Stores. The Promenade was lined with stores. What if the people working didn't know about the monster, and it stepped on their buildings?

Nick ran to the first business he saw—a café, with tables and chairs outside—but just as he reached it, he saw the door being locked from inside. He pounded on the glass frantically, yelling, "You have to get out of here, it's coming!"

The woman locking the door shouted back, "Go away!"

Nick flipped her off, then ran on.

He was at the intersection of Wilshire and 4th when he saw his dream: a woman was struggling to maneuver a stroller through the panicked throngs, crying out as she was buffeted and blocked.

Nick pushed through the crowd, drawing curses and insults in the process, until he reached her. "Forget the stroller—I'll take the baby!"

He started to duck under the stroller's top when he felt agony on his left shoulder, and he realized the woman had hit him. "Leave my baby alone!"

"Owww!"

She was reaching for her cell phone. "I'm calling the police!"

Nick held up his hands, trying to calm her, and backed away. "It's okay; I was just trying to help…"

The baby had turned out to be a dog, anyway.

Nick ran another block, then stopped. He wasn't getting anywhere this way. It was time to really man up. He stopped and turned to face the oncoming monster. The last few runners dodged around him, then it was just him and the 100-foot tall beast, leaving a trail of ebony slime as it came.

"Hey, buddy, get the hell out of there!"

A police car had pulled up behind him, and Nick saw two officers crouching by their vehicle, guns drawn and pointed at the monster…or were they pointed at him?

"It's okay," he shouted back, "I'm going to try to talk to it."

The monster was almost directly over him now. Nick mustered up all the volume he could (maybe he should have paid more attention to those lessons on projecting during acting class) and shouted up, "Please go back to the ocean —"

The monster stepped over Nick and the screaming police. There was a wet *plop,* and Nick realized the creature had dripped stinking sludge on him. He wiped it away from his face, gagging.

"Okay, ya know what? Fuck you!"

He was shrieking at the monster, but the police officers thought Nick was directing his tirade at *them,* and they promptly arrested him on the spot. As they cuffed him and wrestled him into the back of their cruiser, Nick watched the monster continue down Wilshire; and he envied the worldwide coverage he knew the monster would receive.

The monster returned to the sea that evening.

No one knew what it was, or why it had suddenly appeared, or where it went back to, or how it had escaped detection previously. It left behind amazingly little damage — mainly a lot of noxious goo to be cleaned up — and a great deal of speculation. Environmentalists claimed it was a harmless crab, mutated by exposure to the toxins being dumped into the bay. The military labeled it a national terror threat, but were strangely unable to locate it. The Democrats blamed it on the Republicans, and the Republicans blamed it on Satan.

Nick Stadtlinger watched it all from his jail cell. Once witnesses had identified him as the man who'd caused the terrible accident on the PCH, he'd been charged with enough felony offenses to send his bail skyrocketing past what his parents could manage.

His mother, however, visited him with one piece of good news: someone had videotaped his attempt to wrestle the baby (dog) out of the stroller, and the video had gone viral on YouTube. Nick was thrilled.

For two days, Nick Stadtlinger was the most famous asshole in the world.

MONSTERS
of L.A.

THE
DEVIL

THE DEVIL

"C'mon, let's go in."

Jared peered at the Victorian façade, with the quaint gingerbread trim and turrets. He had to admit it was an impressive piece of architecture, especially given that it was situated in the middle of an amusement park and cleverly employed forced perspective to appear bigger than it was.

Ghost House.

"Really? It's not just dumb tricks and spring-loaded cats?"

Maria tugged on his arm. "I can't believe you've never been on it! You love special effects movies, and this is like being right in the middle of one."

Jared tried not to squirm. It was only his second date with Maria (the beautiful Maria, the PoliSci major all the frat boys had bombed out with) and she'd wanted to come here today, to Magic Island, the vast amusement park surrounded, not by water, but by Orange County's labyrinthine freeway network. On Date #1, Jared had discovered that Maria possessed not only an amazing body and beautiful face, but also a sharp mind, a quick wit, and an impressive knowledge of science fiction movies. He hoped there'd be a Date #3, and #4, and #5…

…which was why he couldn't admit that the idea of going through Ghost House terrified him.

It was ridiculous, of course. He was 22, he boxed for fun and could bench press his own weight, had once stood up to a thug trying to rob a convenience store, and the Korean owner had rewarded him with a bottle of Johnny…but the idea of a haunted house ride left him so filled with anxiety that he was queasy and light-headed.

That time at the county fair back home in Oklahoma with his brother…he'd been five and Dennis twelve, and he'd had no choice when Dennis, laughing, had marched him up to "Horror Hotel" and thrust him into the front seat of the sticky, shuddering car. Dennis sat in the seat behind him, and for the next three minutes—as the car rattled along past ragged mannequins, flashes of light and sound, and cartoonish creatures glowing under black lights—Dennis had screamed, poked, jeered, and howled at his terrified sibling. By the time the ride had ended (surely it had been longer than three minutes) Jared knew the world was not a safe place, that no one could be trusted, and that evil things lurked in the dark corners of cheap rides.

"There's not even a line right now…"

Maria was pulling him toward the threshold, but he resisted and she looked at him, perplexed.

"I'm not really a fan of things where people jump out at you…"

"This isn't like that at all. I guarantee it's free of bad actors jumping out screaming 'Boo!'."

God, she was gorgeous. He wished they were together anywhere but here, in this temple to carefully merchandised fantasy, standing before Jared's nightmare. She was gorgeous…and he knew he'd have to go. He'd make the sacrifice (even though she'd never know what this was costing him) and maybe he'd learn something in the process, something about himself and his character, and his courage.

"Okay," he said to her, and her smile affirmed his decision.

It was a Thursday afternoon, and although the rest of Magic Island was thronged with strollers and toddlers, Ghost House was almost empty. They wound quickly through the waiting area and walked in through the open doors of the imitation mansion. A worker dressed in a long black coat and top hat waved them into a side room. There were three others already within. "The show will start in one minute," the worker said, trying to hide his Latino accent behind funereal tones.

The room was decorated as an old-fashioned parlor, with cupboards full of books, dishes, paintings, and mirrors. Overhead, a huge chandelier glowed with artificial light.

A knot of dread was already forming in Jared's gut, but he felt Maria brush against his right arm and tried to concentrate on that. "I thought this was a ride. Do we walk through it, or…?"

"Oh, it's a ride after this part. This just sets everything up."

The worker perched in the doorway through which they'd entered. "Kindly step into the center of the room, and enjoy your visit to Ghost House." He pressed an unseen button, and the door closed, sealing them in.

The lights dimmed, and Jared's anxiety exploded.

The room was abruptly bathed in a soft blue illumination, coming from the mirrors. Jared stared into one and a figure materialized there; it was a middle-aged man, handsome, dapper in a nineteenth-century suit with long coat and vest. "Welcome to Ghost House," he began, his voice resonant, and Jared had to admit the effect was startling—he could still see himself in the mirror, along with the luminescent dandy.

"I'm your host, because this is my house. I'm not just an owner, though; you might say that I'm the master here. The master of what, you're wondering? We are not alone in this house. In fact, this house is rather—" he gestured behind him, and light emanations began to swirl, "—haunted." The glowing eddies took on anthropomorphic form, and the effect was convincing enough that Jared involuntarily glanced over a shoulder. Maria saw his motion, giggled, and reached for his hand.

Jared hoped his palms weren't moist. Maybe she wouldn't notice.

The mirror host continued, specters swimming around him. "And how thoughtful of you to visit today. Unfortunately, there's something about Ghost House you probably didn't know: this house was built without exits. I'm afraid your fate is now sealed, because, you see—you're trapped, and we're just dying to play."

As the host began to roar laughter, the apparition coalesced into a fanged, gaunt face, and launched itself at the mirror. Just as it was about to hit, the lights went completely out, there was the sound of glass shattering, and then an amplified, ear-splitting shriek.

Adrenaline arced through Jared, leaving him filled with a fear so basic (absolute darkness) that for several seconds he lost all awareness of himself.

Then the chandelier returned to life, and a previously hidden door on the room's far side opened. Another worker stood just beyond, waving them out. "Step out, please…this way…"

The other three guests were chuckling, and Maria squeezed Jared's hand tighter. "See? I told you it was good."

Jared hoped his single bark of laughter didn't sound as weak as it felt. "Yeah, that was cool."

They walked down a short, dimly lit hallway lined with portraits of the host. All of the paintings employed some sort of subtle projection that made them move slightly—the eyes followed, or fingers flexed on a hand.

At the end of the hallway was a loading area: small, enclosed cars fashioned like tiny hearses traveled along a hidden track. Watched over by another worker, Jared and Maria stepped into one of the cars, and almost immediately the Host's voice sounded from a speaker just behind them.

"So, you've made it this far, have you? Lean back now, and please pull the safety bar towards you. After all, we wouldn't want you to try to make a run for it, would we?"

Maria pulled the bar down. Jared tried to drink in her glee, forcing himself to emulate her.

The car rounded a corner in the track and they were again plunged into darkness. "Ghost House has over thirty rooms, and they're all quite special. Let's start with something for you music lovers…"

The car turned again; now they were passing through a music room. Lightning flashed in a nighttime sky beyond the windows, spiders crept down tattered wallpaper, and unseen hands played an organ. A tambourine floated just overhead, its miniature cymbals jingling out a rhythm.

"I love that," Maria said, pointing at a candelabra swaying by itself in a corner.

Jared's throat was too dry to answer.

The car continued past various ghoulish tableaux: a sewing room, where clothes mended themselves; a greenhouse, with dog-sized insects scuttling past giant carnivorous plants; a kitchen, with human bones bubbling in a stew pot and a platter of fingers set neatly on a table. The worst, though, was the attic, where ancient storage boxes juddered and tittered.

One burst open and a horrible, open-mouthed demon launched itself up.

Jared's heart leapt into his throat, but he felt shamed when Maria giggled beside him. "Sorry—forgot about him." He realized then he must have crushed her hand in shock.

"No, you were right—this is great."

It was the worst lie of his life.

The car continued past an extravagant outdoor scene of ghosts flitting in and out of tombs and skeletons dancing. Maria delighted in all of it, pointing out a ghost magician who pulled a rabbit skeleton from his hat, and a mummy waltzing with a vampire.

Jared consoled himself by imagining this must be the grand finale, that it was almost over.

The track veered around a crypt and headed for a large, ominous pair of doors. From the speaker behind them, the Host said, "Did you enjoy the party? I'm sure you're sorry to see it end, but it's time to meet your fate."

Over the doors, fiery light revealed a legend carved into stone:

Abandon all hope, ye who enter here.

The doors swung open as the car approached, and a burst of flame made Jared flinch, especially after the sparse lighting of the ride up until now. The car moved through a stone tunnel, but the stone was alive—writhing with forms and faces, the soundtrack full of agonized cries and fiendish shrieks of glee. Ahead, the Host appeared, and Jared couldn't tell if it was a mannequin or a projection.

"I suppose it's only fair that you learn now who your host really is, although I think you already know me…"

There was another eye-searing flash, and the Host's tailored, vintage suit burst into fire. When the flames died down, the Host was clearly revealed as — The Devil. He'd been modeled on every childhood conception, with red skin, horns, a cape, pitchfork and tail. As the car neared and then passed him, Jared saw he had dimension and form, so he assumed it was a robot or a puppet.

"That's my favorite part," Maria whispered next to him.

"Good effect," Jared told her.

The car turned a corner, and Jared nearly melted with relief as he saw an unloading area. The three other guests they'd come in with had already disembarked. Jared's legs felt rubbery as the safety bar flipped up and the car stopped. He stepped out, Maria right behind him. He looked to his right and saw an "Exit" sign, but didn't understand why there was no daylight visible yet.

"There's one more cool little bit," Maria told him.

He tried to act pleased.

Girding himself, he stepped under the "Exit" sign. He saw the other guests stopped a few feet ahead, pointing and laughing at something. At least nothing was jumping out at them.

Jared approached and saw the Devil again, casually seated behind a railing on a rock throne. The trio of guests were bent over something mounted to the railing; it looked like a large book. When they finished, they headed for another door marked "Exit," but this time Jared saw the promise of sunlight. He instinctively headed that way, but felt Maria's touch on his shoulder drawing him back.

"Wait — you'll love this."

Jared hesitated, wanting nothing so much as to be outside again, in safe, cheerful sunlight. He'd made it through Ghost House and hadn't completely embarrassed himself with Maria, who he knew he could easily love. And this, after all—it was just an animatronic figure, wasn't it? A special effect, like the movies he and Maria both loved?

"I see you made it, mortal," the Devil said, in that rich baritone, "and there's a reward waiting for you now. What would you like it to be? Wealth? Fame? Love? Just sign your name in my book and it can be yours."

The figure gestured at the book, and together with Maria, Jared stepped up. There, set carefully on a wooden platform was a huge book, the largest Jared had ever seen. Although the covers weren't visible, Jared could see that the page edges were gold-leafed and the paper had the speckled, creamy look of genuine parchment. There was a pen attached to the book by a length of chain, and dozens of names had already been scribbled on the two visible pages. The book was opened to roughly the middle; Jared couldn't begin to guess how many thousands of pages had already been filled.

Maria playfully lifted the pen. "What should I wish for?"

Jared didn't answer.

He wanted to scream at her, to tell her that something was very wrong here, that the figure of the Devil watching from his granite seat was *too* real, that Ghost House was more than just a simple dark ride elevated to true terror by reliving a childhood trauma, that he believed without question that to sign her name in that book was to give away the most essential part of herself, to relinquish something he hadn't really believed in until now, when he was confronted with its possible loss.

"Maria…I…"

"Oh, here." She extended the pen to him, and he took it with numb fingers.

"You're…not going to sign it?"

She laughed at him. "Silly—I've probably signed it ten times already. Everybody does."

A heaviness he'd never known crushed Jared then. He looked from the pen in his fingers to Maria…

And signed.

She leaned over then and kissed him, and in that instant, Jared knew that their life together would be long and successful, and he would spend most of it trying not to think about why she loved him and what would come after.

They left Ghost House behind and walked hand-in-hand, out to face the blinding California afternoon.

MONSTERS
of L.A.

THE
SLASHER

THE SLASHER

Today I have finally decided to go visit the crack, to at last know, see, what's really in there.

So now I'm sitting on this bus, trying to remember whether I woke up already thinking about the crack, or whether something I saw after I was awake set me off.

I remember rolling out of bed this morning — it's not much of a roll, because the mattress sits right on the floor — and thinking about falling asleep the night before, watching the empty images flicker across the dim television screen. I must've fallen asleep pretty late, 'cause when I woke up the sun was glaring so hard I couldn't see the game shows. First I thought I was supposed to go down to the Unemployment Office today, but then I remembered I'd done that two days ago. As usual, I had nothing to do today.

And then the crack just popped into my head, as if it'd been waiting in the background all last night, while the lights buzzed and the TV crackled and glowed.

I'd been seeing the crack for as long as I could remember — you couldn't miss it, hanging right there in a wall above the Santa Monica beach, passed by a thousand cars a day on their way elsewhere. I don't think anybody except me had ever even noticed the crack, but it had always puzzled me, a rent in the concrete wall holding civilization up and away from the ocean. When I was younger, I used to make the daily pilgrimage to the beach with all the others, but while their faces turned towards the blue, mine was aimed at that black recess. Once, when I was with some friends going down to the beach for a midnight party, I asked them to slow down as we approached, because there was a flashlight in the car, and I'd never seen the crack at night. We slowed to a snail's crawl, and as we passed the crack in the wall, I sent the flashlight beam into it like a thief. The beam swept across what appeared to be rocky sides, an array of rubbish, and maybe even some old furniture, before it was ingested in the far depths. Then we were past it, the beam bouncing harmlessly across even, pale concrete sides. I turned it off, and thought how peculiar it was that after all the times I had been past the crack in the day, this was the first time I had ever actually been able to see into it. I chilled then (and now) as I thought about that ray of light exposing that dark, ignored place, outlining the decay with such eerie precision.

I think that was when I first decided to visit the crack in person some day, and so it is that I now find myself jouncing along in midday heat on the bus, trying to position myself so that my cutoff shorts will take the heat from the ruptured vinyl seat, idly listening to the old woman next to me babbling on. In the midst of another stifling Los Angeles late summer day, she wears a long-sleeved, full-length black dress, of a style I've only seen in old movies. She wanders along in her accented voice about the latest wave of murders, about the cosmic forces in (or out) of our control, about the changing world she can no longer comprehend; in fact, I think the only thing she understands, really grasps, is death. My head nods as she gibbers on, more from the drowsiness inherent in hot busses than from agreement.

At last I begin to feel a slight change in the surroundings, and I realize we are nearing the ocean. I strain up to see out the distant front window, make out the familiar turquoise, and draw myself up, preparing to exit. I see my stop ahead and stand, edge my way past the black-encased knees out into the aisle. The woman appears not to notice, only drones on. The bus creaks to a halt; the doors open with a hydraulic squeal, and I exit. As the big vehicle lumbers off, I glance behind me and notice my former companion move closer to the window and suddenly offer me a wide, toothless grin. I shrug and start down the long street towards the beach.

As I approach the crack, I begin to wish I'd brought along certain things—a flashlight (even though it's broad, glaring daylight) heavier clothes, shoes (I'm barefoot, of course). I can see it now, fifty feet in front of me, from this angle little more than a line bisecting the neatness. It grows rapidly until I'm standing right before it, again wondering why it seems to so completely swallow the sunlight as to render it invisible. I peer into it for a long moment, thinking my eyes will adjust, but I finally realize they will not, and that I have no choice but to enter.

I turn sideways—the crack it only about a foot and a half wide here at the opening, lately I'm thin—and slide over the border. The rocks scrape along my back as I enter, and for some reason I think about edging past the old lady on the bus. Then the crack swiftly widens into a decent ravine, and turning to face it, I take a deep breath of its stale air as if to expand to my full size again. I soon realize that although the street cannot be more than a few yards behind me, I can no longer hear the passing cars clearly; when I turn to look, the outside world has been reduced to a narrow, indistinguishable thread. Again I shrug, and when I turn back to the interior of the crack, I can now plainly make it out, so I guess my eyes have finally adjusted.

The first thing I notice is how much bigger it suddenly seems—the top is now some sixty feet above me and seems to slant off in a constricting steel-gray ribbon, until it is lost entirely. I can't see where the crack ends in the back, and it seems to get bigger the farther into it you go, with smaller cracks and caves punctuating the walls. The floor is damp and slightly mushy, and feels fine to my asphalt-seared toes; I side-step around beer cans, candy wrappers, cigarette butts and little growths of fungi. I notice something bigger ahead, and squinting into the dimness, make out the hulking shape of a rotting couch. I smile down at the rusted springs poking through the ancient, infested material, and I experience a sense of mischievous adventure, the like of which I haven't felt since I was a kid; also, my little discovery is a cool and welcome retreat from the heated insanity outside. I begin to examine the old sofa, wondering how reparable it might be; then I move on past it.

I soon find that the couch is not alone: There is a proliferation of banged wooden chairs, bent metal tables, even a busted white freezer. The only sound now is a steady, and somehow comforting, drip-drip-drip. I collapse gratefully into an aged formerly linen-backed chair.

I don't know how long I've sat here now. The dimness in the crack never changes, and I wonder if I may have fallen asleep. My attention wanders, until for some reason it is caught by an old pair of shoes, the tips of which are just showing from beneath a fallen table. I begin to unthinkingly scrutinize the shoes, which are as corroded as everything else in my crack; I bend down to reach for the shoes, my hand wraps around one, pulls. It seems strangely stuck, and I pull again; the shoe comes free, and I see a white shape left where the shoe had hidden it. Bending close, I stare down in horror as I suddenly realize the shape is a foot, human and fresh, and I look up to see a livid face glaring at me from the other end of the overturned table.

"What the hell ya doin'?" rumbles a craggy voice.

I drop the shoe in surprise, begin to back away. The face floats up in the gloom, and I now see that it is attached to a large body, one over six-and-a-half feet long. The face itself is grizzled with beard stubble, large-nosed with a tracery of broken red veins, and shadowed but lively eyes. The features quiver, then burst into laughter.

"Hey, I'm sorry if I scared ya, but ya gotta admit, turn about's fair play, huh?" He reaches for his shoe, smiling in a friendly way, and I stop retreating. As I watch curiously, he slides the shoe back onto the naked foot, taps his other leg.

"Good thing you didn't pull this other shoe off instead — ya mighta gotten a real scare then." He refuses to elaborate on this until I ask. Then he knocks it solidly and pulls the dirty chino pant leg up.

"Wooden."

I bend down to examine this marvel, and indeed all is wood grain instead of flesh pore. I look up into his old face with the obvious question. He shakes his head, chuckles.

"Naw, I, I might tell ya 'bout it later, but not now. You can call me Redd. And who might you be?"

I name myself, accept his offered hand, am briefly surprised at how long and sharp his fingernails are — I feel their deep indentations in the skin of my palm. He motions me back into my chair, then flops down into a mess that may once have been an overstuffed chair, wipes his greasy forehead with the dingy, blue baseball cap he wears. I tentatively gesture at the surroundings.

"Do you live here?"

"I do right now, I reckon." He continues to grin at me, and I wonder at how clean and strong his teeth look.

"So, uh, Redd, what's it like to live here?"

He eyes me with a perception that makes me feel unclothed before him. "You wouldn't be here unless you already knowed the answer to that."

I nod, understanding that he's right. "Doesn't anybody else ever come in here?"

"Nope. You're the first one ever. That's why I like ya—I don't much like most people on the outside." He gestures, incorrectly I think, behind him.

"Why not?" I ask.

"Why not what?"

"Why don't you like most people on the outside?"

"'Cause they don't like me, I reckon."

I relax, smile at the thought of leading this pleasant old eccentric on, feeling like one of those adults on TV commercials goading on some precocious seven-year-old. "I like you. Why wouldn't they?"

He appears to seriously consider this before replying. "Maybe it ain't me they don't like, so much as things I done."

"Like what?" I again notice the steady dripping noise, begin to feel a vague discomfort at the sound.

He grins finally, leans forward. "I'll tell ya what—you really wanna hear how I lost my leg?"

I nod.

"Lost it in the hospital."

He leans back, his motion inviting my questions, and for the first time now, the probability hits me that this is all a hoax, a bizarre joke being played on a gullible invader of his realm. I decide to play along, for a while, anyhow.

"Hospital? Veterans Hospital, maybe, a war injury?"

He shakes his head no, delighted with this guessing game.

"An accident, then."

"You might say that!" He bursts into laughter, great explosions that shake dust-falls of clay out of the ravine walls. "I'll give ya a hint—a different kind of hospital."

Perplexed, I think for a moment, until my expression mirrors my arrived-at answer, and he nods, pleased.

"You got it now. Y'know, I can't remember much that happened to me afore that, but I sure do remember that hospital. Do you remember a lot of things that happen to you?"

This strange question makes me uneasy, and my shoulders twist in partial response. "Yeah..."

"You remember stuff that happened to you a long time ago?"

"You mean like when I was a kid?"

He bristles at this query, drawing himself up until he towers over me even though we are both seated; he glowers at me suspiciously, and I know now that this is no prankster playing games.

"You like kids?" he asks.

I answer instinctively, "Not much."

He eases back down, taps me amiably on the arm. "See, I knew I liked you, 'cause you ain't like those people. They all think kids is somethin' great. Not me. I think they're mostly just too loud, so I shut 'em up."

I shiver, and looking up, see the sky above the crack has gone indigo with the setting of the sun. I return my gaze to the gleaming eyes watching me with anticipation, and know I can't evade them. "You—shut—"

"Yeah, it's pretty easy, ya know, all ya need's a pillow and—hell, they can't fight back, so it's easy, only takes a minute or so, then they're quiet. But people don't like quiet, so they put me away."

I find I am quite speechless by now, can only sit…and wait.

He pauses, then raps a fist against his forehead. "Oh, right, you wanna hear 'bout my leg. A'most forgot. See, the doctors and all what run this hospital, they don't like me much either, I guess, though I don't know what I coulda done to them; so they decides they're gonna really lock me away, y'know, by m'self in one a' them padded cells, in a—now what the hell is it—yeah, a straitjacket."

He pronounces that last word with such enunciated venom that I recoil for a beat, wonder if my face looks as cold as it feels.

"So there I am, sittin' in that rubber room one day—'bout all you can do is sit, y'know—when the door opens, only it ain't my doctor, and it sure ain't no nurse, it's these three guys, and they look kinda, well, crazy, I guess. An' I say, 'Where's my doctor?', an' one a 'em says, 'Where he can't interfere,' so I starts to screamin'. I put up a ruckus loud 'nough to raise the dead, an' these three just stands there an' laughs, an' finally one yells, 'Scream all ya want, freak, they won't come t' help.'"

He leans back, memory clouding his features. "So I stops, looks 'em square in the eye, an' says, 'So what the hell you want?' One says, 'We found out what you done, an' we don't much like it, I'm 'fraid,' then this big one who ain't said a word steps forward, an' 'fore I know it the other two has grabbed me so's I can't move a muscle, grinnin' like mad dogs all the while, an' then the big one he pulls out a knife, only he just uses it to slit my trouser leg off; then he tosses it inta the corner, an' he kneels down. One a' the other ones holdin' me down gestures at that big droolin' face down by my feet, and says—I could never forget it—'Jed's hungry.'"

The gleam leaves his eyes, giving the impression that the crack has now been plunged into total darkness. I experimentally tense the tendons in my thighs, find that my knees will still support weight, begin slowly inching my tortuous way up off my seat. I am suddenly paralyzed as his voice comes again, softly, but enough to shatter the precious silence.

"The doctors come 'bout the time Jed there was up through my knee, an' they took 'em 'way, an'—well, y'know, maybe it weren't such a bad thing, 'cause then, see, the doctors they felt sorry for me, and soon's I was healed and fitted, they let me out, even gimme a little somethin' to live on—not enough, though."

My heart skips a pulse as he leaps up, but it is only to dig beneath the tattered seat cushion, rummage up a newspaper, already yellowing and eaten away in places. He thrusts it out to me, and for some reason—it must not be as dark as I thought it was—I can read it perfectly. The headline, which I recognize as being less than a month old, screams 13TH VICTIM TORN APART BY SANTA MONICA RIPPER. He pats the paper proudly, says, "They may not like me, but at least they know who I am. 'Course this one's old—been four since, two I don't think they even found yet, or least not all a 'em."

I push up out of the chair on the strength of arteries pumping ice water, start backing away, realize I don't know where the opening is any more. He continues, following me jovially.

"See, they gimme some money, but nothin' to do, so I got kinda bored, ya know? And babies, well, I thought, there's just as many loud adults as babies, right?"

I nod desperately, running my hands along the wall behind me as a guide, since my eyes refuse to leave the figure before — behind? — me. He frowns now, and I try to move faster, scraping my hands badly.

"You seemed like such a nice person. Now why you wanna leave in such a hurry? I was just gettin' started."

He reaches behind him, magically produces a smeared piece of metal, which used to support the back of a lawn chair, but has now been cleverly shaped and sharpened into a home-made cleaver. My legs abruptly cease to work, and I discover that one of my feet has slipped out from under me, slipped on something wet, something odorous leaking out thickly from an indentation in the bottom of the crack's wall. He takes a step so close that, over the other smells, I catch the sullied iron in his hands.

"See, I didn't tell you the resta the story. When ol' Jed was down there workin' on my leg, the other two that were with him...well, they took a piece Jed had pulled away, and they held my head down, and they made me...funny thing is, seems I developed a likin' for the taste."

He smiles then, looking around the crack. "I like it here," he says in a hush.

But all I can hear is that damned drip-drip-drip.

MONSTERS
of L.A.

THE KILLER
CLOWN

THE KILLER CLOWN

"Did you *really* have to wear a clown costume?"

John snorted in disbelief. "You're kidding right? Christ, Mel, I'm not even wearing a clown face."

Melanie knew it was true — he claimed to be making a "political statement" by wearing a red-and-blue clown suit with a rubber mask aping the face of his current least favorite presidential candidate — but she was still made uneasy by the oversized yellow shoes, the padded waist, the red polka dots like huge blood splatters.

"You know how I feel about…clowns."

Even saying the name made Melanie shiver. As for John — of course he knew. On their second date he'd brought over a favorite horror movie to watch, in which a child's nightmare was dominated by a leering, white-greasepainted clown, and Melanie'd had to leave the room. Later, when John had turned the movie off and apologized, she'd told him about her Uncle Larry, who'd been obsessed with clowns (his work office was a pink abattoir of circus memorabilia, and more than once Melanie had wondered how Larry's employees had tolerated it) and who'd insisted on appearing at all of Melanie's birthday parties dressed as "Hoho the Hobo," a monstrous creation of oversized lips, bulbous red nose, and filthy crushed hat. "Hoho" enjoyed diving abruptly into a child's screaming face, or suddenly popping up before them with his "exploding cigar" gag, and more than one of Melanie's small friends had fled her parties in tears and avoided Melanie thereafter. By the time she was ten, Melanie had a phobia of clowns, no friends, a dislike of birthdays, and a thorough hatred of Uncle Larry. When he'd died of a heart attack two years later, Melanie had secretly felt tremendous joy.

"I know, Mel, but…well, it's Halloween. You're probably gonna be seeing a lot of clowns where we're going."

He was right. They were heading south on Vineland, away from innocent trick-or-treaters and the cozy little two-bedroom shack in Sun Valley, over the hills and into West Hollywood, for its annual celebration. A million visitors were expected this year, and Melanie figured probably a tenth of them would be dressed as clowns. There'd be, in other words, a lot of clowns. And drag queens. But mainly clowns.

If they hadn't made plans to meet up with John's friends at the Pacific Design Center, she would've begged him to turn around. Maybe she still could. He could drop her off, go without her. After all, they were *his* friends. And at least one of them was probably dressed as a clown.

"John…"

He cut her off; he probably knew what she'd been about to say. Three years of marriage had given them that pseudo-telepathic shared ability. "Hey, did I tell you how cute you look, matey? Arrrggghhh." He spun the last word out into a lustful appreciation.

Mel glanced down at her pirate outfit, and had to admit that she *did* look good in the swashbuckling black hot pants and the ruffled blouse, with the fake parrot wired to one shoulder and the real (sheathed) Japanese sword that her grandfather had brought back from The Big One. "Thanks," she mumbled.

Maybe she could make it through this evening after all. It was only one night. And Halloween was supposed to be fun, wasn't it? She was a pirate queen, damn it. She'd have fun tonight. Clowns would walk the plank.

"Oh, crap, I forgot that wine Brian wanted me to bring." They were supposed to get together after the West Hollywood event; Brian was a complete snob, but he did own a beautiful home in the Hollywood hills, which was the closest Melanie ever got to L.A.'s high life.

John glanced around, spotted a cross street sign, and steered the car into the left lane. "I think there's a liquor store right up here."

Melanie thought for a second—and her blood went cold.

Big Top Liquor. Home of the thirty-foot-tall neon clown sign.

It was coming into view now, as John pulled into the left-hand turn lane. A huge, glowing thing of terror, with a face that was likelier to inspire bad dreams than purchases. Just driving by that sign had brought a chill to her in the past; now, pulling up beneath it to park, she was speechless with dread.

Big Top Liquor. She was here, on Halloween, sitting next to a clown. She couldn't move.

John finished pulling into a space, turned off the ignition and leaned over towards her. "I know, hon, and I'm sorry; but it's the biggest liquor store between here and West Hollywood, and you know I love you…"

"Just make it quick," she said, waving a nerveless hand in the direction of the store. She made the mistake of glancing out the window, and saw the sign off to her right. Even though she was beneath it, at an angle, she could swear the illuminated white face was staring down at her, with its wild eyes and snaggle toothed gaping mouth and—

"Mel!"

She jerked, startled. "What?"

"I said, are you sure you don't want to come with me?"

Melanie glanced out the window again and weighed her options: She could wait alone, in the car, eyes tightly closed against the gleeful thirty-foot-tall menace just outside, or she could go into the store with John and be out of sight of it for a few moments.

"Okay."

John climbed out of the car and came around to open her door. He was still gallant, even after three years of marriage (and even while dressed in a clown suit) and she felt a tiny bit better for it. She took his hand and let him lead her into the store while she carefully avoided glancing up at the sign, sure that if she did it would be turning to follow, pulling loose from post and wires.

They passed through the front glass door into the large store, aisles stocked with bottles extending before them. To the left of the entrance was the sales counter.

Behind the counter was a clown.

Melanie's heart skipped a beat and her stomach clenched in terror. This was a real clown, with a ludicrous costume and a painted face. He wore a bright green shirt with orange suspenders and a red bow tie; his face was completely covered in white, mouth outlined in black, head crowned by an outrageous crimson fright wig. He stared at her silently; even though his makeup centered on a massive smile, beneath the paint his mouth wasn't turned up. His eyes measured her, making her feel like the victim of a crime about to happen. He didn't move, didn't speak…just stared, unblinking.

"Mel…" John was beside her, tugging at her gently. "C'mon, honey."

She let him pull her along into the store, away from the counter; she felt the clown's exaggerated eyes on her back and resisted the urge to duck down and crawl.

"I'm really sorry," John whispered, "I didn't think…fucking Big Top Liquor on Halloween. I should've guessed somebody'd be in a clown costume here."

Melanie didn't answer; she couldn't.

"I'll make this quick, I promise. We're looking for a char-donnay put out by a company called Payasos Vineyards…"

Melanie tried to force her attention to the bottles ranked on shelves around her. They were in the aisle of red wines. Mer-lots, cabernets, pinot noirs…she was surrounded by elegant vintages the color of blood.

John had moved away from her to the next row, and Mela-nie wandered down towards the rear of the store, away from the front counter. Ahead of her were the cold sections, glass doors protecting icy bottles of beer and wine. She forced herself to be practical; maybe John's wine was here, and it would be better chilled anyway. She stepped up close to the glass, found several sections of white wines, began examining the labels, looking for Payasos—

A clown face peered at her from the frigid darkness behind the bottles.

Melanie gasped and staggered back, colliding with a rack of chips. She caught herself on the rack and kept it from going down, although several bags behind her crinkled loudly. John

213

was beside her instantly, grabbing her arm, concerned, steadying her.

"What—?"

She raised a shaking hand. "In there, staring at me, a… face…"

John looked where she was pointing, stepped up to the door, reached out for the handle.

"John, don't—!"

He smiled reassuringly. "It's okay…" He opened the door and looked inside. Melanie felt the refrigerated air rolling out around him. He peered inside for a few seconds, then turned back to her. "See? Nothing—"

A gloved hand reached out from between the shelves and found John's throat. His reassurance was choked off instantly as he was pulled back to crash against the bottles. His eyes widened, fingers flew to the puffy white glove wrapped around his neck. He was yanked back again and bottles flew, crashing at Melanie's feet as John was pulled into the frosty space behind the doors. Metal clanged loudly, wine fizzled onto the tiled floor, and John was gone. After a second, the glass door swung slowly to, its rubber-sealed edges guaranteeing anything behind would stay sealed in cold.

Melanie stared for a second, stunned, then her legs moved on their own. She spun, started stumbling towards the front. Her eyes sought out the counter clown, but he'd vanished. She focused entirely on the door, on the way out, almost there, reaching out—

Her hands thudded against a locked door. "Fuck! Open the goddamn door!"

A laugh roared out next to her.

Melanie screamed and turned to see the counter clown, no

longer silent, but now leaning forward over the counter and screeching at her, high-pitched cackles that sent electrical arcs of fear jagging throughout her body. She staggered back as the clown leaned forward, his black mouth tilting impossibly up and up at the corners, his eyes as red as his nose.

She turned and ran, staggering, barely aware of containers she knocked over in her flight, crashing to the floor behind her. She found herself back at the coolers, where John had been taken—

Behind the glass were no bottles now, but dozens of clown faces, outlined in the darkness, peering out at her. There were all kinds of clown faces—some with color only around their mouths, some with full masks, some with faces that looked half eaten away by malicious glee, teeth filed to tiny points…

The clowns stepped forward, pushing the doors out, lining up in the store before her, a dozen of them. They faced her, some cackling, some tittering, all grinning in wicked antici-pation. Their hands—cartoon gloves, half-finger mittens, or simply bare—twitched, flexing.

They wanted Melanie.

She was panting, felt her vision giving way to sheer hyste-ria, tried to think. She backed away, looking for a way out, a sanctuary—and the laughter was right behind her, almost in her ear. She jerked around and saw the counter clown behind her, blocking the way out.

Melanie was trapped.

Her hands flew over her own arms, her sides, wrapping around her. The cooler clowns advanced, taking their time, relishing her terror. She felt the weight of the counter clown behind her, pressing in. Her hands ran desperately down her side—

And found the sword. A real sword, with a deadly blade. She'd cut her finger on it once, just sliding it out of the wooden sheath. John had tried to convince her not to wear it tonight, that she could be arrested for carrying a deadly weapon; but she'd liked the way it looked hanging from her scarlet sash, so she'd kept it on, defiantly—

She pulled it out now and lifted it, letting the clowns see the glinting, lethal metal blade. This was no plastic Halloween toy, no child's prop—

A clown with a spinning bow tie and bowler hat dressed in flowers lunged.

Melanie closed her eyes and swung the sword. She felt an impact, and then looked:

One of the clown's arms had been severed at the shoulder. The limb, still clad in canary yellow shirtsleeve, spun away. From the abrupt stump spilled something pink and viscous, barely liquid, more like…cobwebs.

Or cotton candy.

The clowns hesitated in their advance now, and Melanie's fear was forced back slightly. Maybe she could still escape from this. Maybe her grandfather's violent gift would now spell her freedom—

The counter clown wrapped his arms around her from behind. She struggled, battered his arms with the sword's hilt. His grip didn't loosen. Melanie juggled the sword in her right hand, managed to reverse her grip, and thrust blindly backwards. She felt the sword embed in something solid, heard the shrieking laughter turn to agony; and she was free. She turned to see that she'd stabbed the counter clown through the side, in the rib cage. While he was clutching at himself, surprised and enraged, she swept the sword in an arc that carried through his neck. The clown was decapitated, his head still wearing a look of astonishment as it flew through the air to crash into a shelf of spiced rum. More of the gooey ichor gushed from the neck, as the body fell to the floor.

Melanie stepped gingerly over the headless corpse, trying to avoid the pink puddles, inching her way backwards towards the front door. She didn't know if she could cut her way out or not, but at least maybe she could batter the doors, call for help, find a phone, *something*—

"Melanie."

John.

Relief rushed through her as she heard his voice, behind her, near the exit. He'd gotten away, she knew he wasn't dead, and together they could escape this place, the clowns—

She saw him, and her relief turned to stone instantly.

John was a clown now.

He still wore the same costume, with the huge yellow shoes and the red splotches, but now his face had been painted, an orange mouth turned down and sad, triangular eyes. His own thick brown hair that she'd always loved, had been teased up and out in all directions.

The red smeared on his throat wasn't paint.

"This is where they're born," he said, his voice hollow, rasping at the ends of syllables.

Melanie felt tears track down her cheeks, and she wiped them away, hurriedly, trying to keep her eyes clear. "John, what…?"

"The clowns. This is where they all come from. Once a year, on Halloween. All the evil clowns in the world are birthed right here. From people like us."

"You're not making sense, John—"

He paused to squeeze a bicycle horn he now held in one hand. It emitted a loud, irritating HONK. "That's true. Sense is overrated. The clowns know that. That's why they're perfect for this world."

Melanie edged forward, toward him. "Let me go, John. I'll just leave, I'll…"

He shook his head, gave the horn another squeeze. "It's better that you stay."

"Why? Why is it better?"

"Because," John said, waving the horn at the coolers behind her, "you can join us."

Hands reached around Melanie then and plucked the sword from her grip. She heard it clatter to the ground, discarded, but was crying too much to reach for it. She struggled, but dozens of hands gripped her now, pulling her back towards the coolers, where she would be reborn. She wondered if she'd have to wait until next Halloween, or if she'd be able to join John tonight. She wondered where they'd go, if they'd show up at birthday parties and create new, terrified generations.

She gave out one last scream, and then the cold air enveloped her.

MONSTERS
of L.A.

THE URBAN
LEGEND

THE URBAN LEGEND

CHAPTER 1

"Los Angeles is striving for an image that is Los Angeles.
We want more air and space in our buildings."

—Architect Paul R. Williams
(speech at art commission, 1963)

It started with a lizard.

Strange that I'm just now remembering that. Out of all the things that happened that day—that day I'm choosing as the beginning—what I'm remembering is a lizard, a small brown lizard scuttling up the side of the construction pit's wall. I looked at it running for shelter, and I thought, *Won't do any good. They'll start pouring concrete here in an hour, and you'll be dead.* I felt a kind of distant pity for it, but of course, feeling for another creature required me to see past my own wall of emotion, which was miles thick that morning.

The path down was rough gravel, and I slipped when I looked up at the lizard. Fortunately Sam, right behind, caught my elbow and steadied me. I'd almost forgotten he was there, and when I glanced at him, his eyes were concerned beneath the construction hard hat.

"Gil, you okay?" he asked.

I nodded, a purely reflexive gesture…then caught myself. It was a lie, and Sam deserved better.

I wasn't okay. I'd never been less okay in my life.

I almost turned, then, and marched up out of that pit, because I was about to lose something in front of Sam that I didn't want him to see. He was my friend Sam, true, and I knew he cared about me…but he was also Professor Samuel Dorian West, renowned author, my former teacher, now my boss, the perfect distinguished bearded scholar, and a man twice my age. I was 23, a graduate student in Folklore Studies, a woman in a competitive academic world where emotion was a weakness. I'd be damned if I'd cry in front of him.

"Sorry, I…" I could hear the husk in my own voice, and I tried to clear it before I continued. "Maggie left me last night."

There—it was out. The enormity of it hit as the words left me, and I suddenly didn't care who saw my tears. Because Maggie had left last night, taking my happiness—the happiness I thought we'd shared for a year—with her. Of course I knew Maggie had met someone else recently—a mid-level film company executive named Deena, older, more sophisticated, with money—but I'd stupidly believed it to be only infatuation.

Until last night, as Maggie had packed one bag and said she'd be back for the rest when I wasn't in the apartment.

Sam said something to me, something apologetic and kind about waiting in the car, and his voice brought me back from thoughts of the terrible night, a night without sleep, hoping she'd return, knowing she wouldn't. I wiped my eyes, then saw my friend Jim Straycloud waiting for us, twenty feet farther down, looking at me.

Deep breaths, concentration…

I looked up, trying to calm myself, but what I saw didn't help. The morning sun hadn't yet cleared the buildings that towered over the sides of the construction pit, and to the left The Castle crouched in silhouette, a great brick-and-iron predator. I was well acquainted with the history of the place—I practically had to be, given how much Sam talked about it in the new book—but I'd never liked it; even though it'd long ago been converted to artists' lofts, there was still something too Victorian about it for modern-day Southern California. Just to the south, I could hear rush hour traffic flowing into downtown L.A., and the cloudless sky was already tinged with the brown of smog…and I knew where I was. My home, the native land I'd been born to, a rare second generation Angeleno.

"Gil…?" That was Jim, calling up to me.

"Coming." I shrugged off Sam's hand (but tried to offer him a thankful smile first) and started down the path again.

We were descending a pebbly trail carved into the earth by bulldozers now sitting idle at the bottom of the excavation. Jim approached a far wall, and I finally spotted our reason for being here:

He crouched by a small hole, set just a yard above the floor of the pit. The hole was only a few feet in diameter, with a pile of stones nearby indicating that parts of the embankment had crumbled around it.

"That's it, eh?" Sam walked past on my right, and I heard the excitement in his voice.

Jim (sweet, hard-working Jim, who I'd dated twice before Maggie had arrived, and who I was still friends with) had called this morning at just past 8 a.m. and told me about the construction site he was working on in downtown L.A. They were about to lay the foundation for a new parking structure, when they'd spotted the hole in the wall. Quick inspection with a flashlight had revealed this was no unmapped sewer main or natural tunnel, but rather something old and obviously manmade.

"I thought of that guy you TA for, the one who's the big expert on local history," Jim had told me on the cell phone, while I'd struggled to understand something that didn't begin and end with Maggie's departure.

"Professor West," I'd answered, barely interested.

Jim had gone on to explain that he could only hold up the crews for a short time, unless the tunnel was a major find.

"We'll be there in an hour," I'd told him; then I called Sam.

During the drive, Sam had speculated, "My God, what if it's the Chinese?"

For years, Sam had researched rumors of a series of tunnels built beneath 19th century Los Angeles. Every Chinatown in the U.S. had supposedly had them, but Sam had finally ruled the notion a mere fiction, perpetrated largely by prejudiced non-Asians who'd claimed the tunnels had housed prostitution and opium dens. However, Sam couldn't completely discount histories that claimed L.A.'s Chinese had used the tunnels to hide from bloodthirsty mobs during the notorious 1871 riot that had claimed the lives of 18 residents of Chinatown.

Sam and I joined Jim, who held a flashlight up and aimed it into the dark interior. "See the brick in there? And there's some other stuff, can't quite make it out…"

I tried to peer past Jim's elbow, and saw the light beam picking out dusty brick lining tunnels that were just wide and tall enough to allow passage. Farther down the narrow way, which extended off an unknown distance, the fading light picked out some objects on the floor; but they were too dim to define.

"Can I have that?" Sam didn't wait for Jim to hand him the light; instead he simply grabbed it and thrust it farther into the tunnel. After a few seconds, he held it back to me. "Take this."

I did—and had to jump back as Sam began pummeling the sides of the opening with his bare hands.

"Professor—!"

Sam ignored the detritus that rattled off his hardhat as he continued to widen the hole. Jim watched uncertainly. "I'm not sure that's a good idea—this whole side could give way—"

Something about that hole in the earth, widening fitfully under Sam's efforts, gave me a small shiver. Maggie wouldn't have shivered; she was like Sam—fearless, energetic. I felt more like the tiny brown lizard—desperate to find the nearest place to hide.

A few seconds later, Sam had an opening wide enough to haul himself through. Once he was inside and on his feet again, he knelt down toward me. "Coming?"

Despite my unease, I accepted his offered hand and let him pull me up into the tunnel. I turned the flashlight on again and offered it to Sam. He took it, swinging the beam side to side, running fingers along the brick.

"What do you see?" Jim asked from outside.

"Nothing yet. We're going further in."

I followed Sam, making sure my own hard hat was secured. The brick, its color dull rose beneath layers of decades, was cracked and crumbling, and we could feel the vibration of street life above. My throat was dry, and I was wiping my sweaty hands on my jeans as Sam walked toward one of the objects we'd only glimpsed from outside. It was an old-fashioned wooden barrel, still largely intact, only a few of the planks rotted away, leaving jagged gaps. Sam knelt by the barrel and examined it until he saw something that made him cry out, exhilarated.

"Ha! Look at this!"

I moved around to the other side of the barrel and looked where Sam was pointing:

There were Chinese characters written on the side of the barrel. I forced a smile, trying to echo his joy of discovery. "You were right."

He nodded and turned away. A few yards farther down, we found a ceramic vase, obviously old and of Asian origin. There were moldering wooden crates, more barrels, the remains of tools. There was obvious trash—discarded bottles, a few shreds of paper, an urn blackened from years of tobacco-stained spit. We came across two doorways, both long ago bricked over.

Sam remembered his camera and pulled it from a pocket, then started snapping away. "Do you get what this material means, Gillian?"

I waited, knowing the question was rhetorical. I'd worked for Sam long enough now (two months) to know that he often tested out ideas on me before committing them to paper, and that he required a response only when something wasn't completely clear.

"The historical accounts were right: Look at the things left in this tunnel. I'll bet that barrel once held water. We've seen bottles, crates—not the things you'd expect if these tunnels had been used for any illicit purposes. No; these were used for transporting goods between shops and hiding from the white man."

The camera flash momentarily blinded me, and I flinched and rubbed my puffy eyes. When I could see again, Sam was twenty feet away, staring at something to the right of the tunnel.

"What is *this*…?"

I joined him, and found he was looking at a large archway set into the brick. The edges of the archway were inscribed with more Chinese characters, but they weren't in mere black ink; no, they glittered in the light beam, raised and bulky. Sam reached out to wipe the thick layer of dust away, and I asked, "Those letters aren't real gold, right?"

"Actually, I think they are." The tiny electronic *click* of the camera echoed loudly in the tunnel.

Then it wasn't the gold characters that I was looking at; it was the doors.

Set into the arch beneath the gilt inscription were two huge wooden doors, with a still-sturdy cross bar laid against them. Something about the doors made my throat tighten even more, and I wanted very badly to turn and run, just get out of there, away.

"Professor…?"

Sam was busy wiping grime from the letters and photographing them in sequence. He responded only with a preoccupied grunt.

"Why are these doors barred?"

He didn't look up from the camera's LCD. "To keep anyone on the other side from getting in. Like a lynch mob."

"So why aren't all the other doors barred, too?"

That stopped him. He lowered the camera, considering. "Now that's a very good question. Let's see if we can answer it."

He slid the camera back into a pocket, and started pulling at the cross bar.

The bar was heavy, and he had to use his weight to leverage it out. For some reason I couldn't explain, the door unnerved me more than anything else in the tunnel; and I nearly reached out to stop him. "Are you sure we should do that? I mean, what if there's…I don't know, gas or something on the other side…?"

"Then hold your breath." He gave me a quick grin, then yanked the bar out and set it aside. There was a rusting ring in the center of the door, and Sam grasped it, pulling. The door opened out a few inches, the scraping noise it made against the rough floor sounding like a dozen fingernails on a chalkboard. It seemed to take minutes, hours, as Sam steadily pulled, and there was a slight *whoosh* and the scent of mildew as the door opened. Finally, it stood far enough ajar that Sam was able to squeeze through while I waited, holding my breath to listen.

After a few deadly quiet seconds, I couldn't wait any longer. "Professor…?"

His voice came from the other side of the door. "There's a passage here, but…" He trailed off.

"But what?"

Sam didn't answer, but the flashlight beam swung to and fro.

Something glittered, something at my feet I hadn't noticed before. I bent to pick it up, and felt a small piece of cool stone. The light turned away and it was dark again, the only illumination coming from the now-distant tunnel mouth. I held the piece up so it was silhouetted, and made out some string, something like a tassel, and the stone—perhaps two inches wide, carved into the shape of an animal head, flat, long, low nostrils like…

A lizard.

"Gil…?"

I jumped and nearly dropped the piece as Sam appeared from behind the door again. "Wherever that went, it caved in long ago. Only goes a few feet back now." Sam saw the object in my hand then. "What's that?"

I passed it to him, and when he played the light on it I saw the red thread, colorful against the green of the stone—jade. "I found it out here."

"Some sort of charm. It was probably originally hung from the top of the archway here. Looks like a…"

Sam's brow creased—and then he began to laugh. The laughter bothered me as much as the doorway, because I knew its source.

The Lizard People story.

"Professor West…we should probably go talk to Jim…"

He pushed past me, practically jittering with adrenaline. "Goddamn right we should. The construction's going to have to stop for a while, I'm afraid."

As I followed him out, glad to return to the sunlight and smog, I thought again of the small brown lizard I'd seen scamper up the walls of the site.

Looks like you got a reprieve after all, you lucky little bastard.

Chapter 2

"One of the most curious episodes in the history of Los Angeles centers around the persistent urban legend of G. Warren Shufelt and the Hopi Lizard People. Was Shufelt just a Depression Era conman with an outrageous scam, a misguided engineer who was himself victim of a hoax perpetrated by a so-called Indian chief, or an authentic genius who uncovered the secret of a lost tribe of lizard people living beneath Los Angeles? With the aid of a device that he claimed could detect gold at a distance via radio waves, Shufelt began digging around Los Angeles in 1933... and had vanished by 1934, probably with an angry investor or two on his tail."

— From Samuel West's *The Secret History of Los Angeles*
(work in progress)

Three days later, Sam's friend in the Linguistics Department, Kelvin Tsui, offered up his translation of the inscription surrounding the double doors. Sam was disappointed to be told that the characters related little more than a date of construction (1864) and the name of the Chinatown "Benevolent Society" that had financed the tunnels.

Five days later, Sam lost his fight to save the tunnel for posterity, and work resumed on pouring the foundation for a new parking structure. I got a properly apologetic call from Jim, and promised we'd do lunch soon.

And a week later, my shock had moved into the rage phase of "Life After Maggie."

I hadn't seen Maggie since. On the second day, I'd returned from work to find a key, a check, and a forwarding address on the kitchen table. No apology, no offer of friendship or show of concern, just a street that I recognized as belonging to a chic area of Echo Park that had recently undergone serious gentrification. Maggie had traded up.

On a Thursday morning, I walked into Sam's office for the usual morning conference, only to find him more preoccupied than usual.

"Got anything going this afternoon? Say, around 3 p.m.?"

"Just some study." Truthfully, I'd planned to buy a bottle of white wine on the way home and drink, graduate degree be damned.

"I've got an appointment you might find interesting. And to tell you the truth, I could use some backup."

He told me: He'd received a call yesterday from a movie studio executive who was interested in developing an idea around some of the folklore Sam had described in his book *Crying Women and Cat Spirits: Mexican Folklore North of the Border*. Sam was more than a little surprised by the call, since the book had been mainly sold to libraries and universities… but, smelling movie money, he'd agreed.

"Oh…" I rolled the idea of going with him around for a moment, and for the first time in a week felt a shimmer of interest in something that didn't involve grieving. "I'd like to run home and change first…"

"Well, I think you look great right now, but—sure, fine."

As I walked across campus to the apartment, I started wondering (not for the first time) about my mentor. He was a 50-something bachelor, the kind of guy who still ate burritos for lunch and ended up wearing a lot of the meal, and for a while I'd assumed that work had always taken precedence for Sam West, over relationships. But lately I'd begun to wonder if he didn't feel something more than a teacher's recognition of a student where I was concerned; I thought he might be interested in me, and I wasn't sure yet how I felt about that. Two weeks ago I would have laughed it off, had someone else suggested it, but…not now.

By 3:45 p.m., Sam was guiding his jeep down the twisting maze of the parking structure beneath an immense black tower in the San Fernando Valley. I'd gotten a laugh out of Sam by suggesting that the 15-story building bore an uncanny resemblance to the monolith in *2001: A Space Odyssey*.

At two minutes until 4 we stepped out of the elevator onto the 15th floor, finding ourselves in a spacious lobby tiled in black marble, with soft concealed lighting and film projections on the walls running trailers from upcoming movies. Behind a desk the size of my living room, sat a perfectly coiffed young woman who offered a practiced and insincere smile.

"Hi," Sam said, pausing before the desk, "Sam West and Gillian Keffler. I have an appointment with Don Edwards."

"Sure. If you'll just take a seat, Mr. Edwards will be with you in a moment."

She waved a manicured hand at a leather couch wedged into a corner, near a dark metal water sculpture, then she spoke softly into a headset.

I sat, trying not to stare like a bumpkin tourist, but it was hard; even though I was a native, I was as much in awe of movie glamour as anyone; and I sure wasn't used to this kind of ostentation. "This guy's not some mid-level exec," I half-whispered to Sam.

"No kidding." Sam's surprise was obvious and genuine. I realized he had also succumbed to the thrill of Hollywood, and I felt a little stab of affection for him just then.

A few minutes later, we were ushered into an office that made the lobby look like a cheap motel room. One entire wall was glass, with a spectacular view of the Valley. There were bookcases, a fully stocked bar, a huge plasma screen television, and a desk that looked more like pop art. The desk had been situated near the windows, forcing anyone sitting before it to squint against the sunlight.

Don Edwards stood as we came in, offering his hand. I took it first, and had the uncomfortable sensation of gripping the soft underbelly of a predator. The man was young, blandly handsome, and dressed in suit jacket and casual shirt — despite the stifling heat of the office. I saw Sam tug at his collar and knew he was also uncomfortable, but Edwards hadn't so much as popped a bead of sweat.

After introductions we sat, and were both flinching from the bright wall of glass behind Edwards.

Deliberate, I realized. *This guy's a prick. Welcome to Hollywood.*

"So, Sam," he started, and there was an odd, measured aggression in his voice, "tell me what you know about The Lizard People of Los Angeles."

I looked at Sam, who blinked in surprise. "The Lizard People? I'm sorry, but I didn't realize…I haven't covered them in a book yet…"

"But you're working on that right now, aren't you?"

Sam glanced at me uncertainly, as if signaling for help.

"Well," I ventured, "you *did* post a blog about that part of your book…"

"Ah." Sam returned his attention to Edwards. "I suppose a film based on that legend would be interesting."

"Our movie actually centers on the crazy engineer. Shufelt."

Between the excessive temperature and the conversation, my head was swimming. It was like there was some subtext here I wasn't grasping, as if this were a game and I didn't know the rules.

"Oh, Shufelt." Sam nodded, smiling. "He was quite the character."

"What do you know about him?"

Sam shrugged. "He's a bit enigmatic. I mean, there are all the news reports from 1933, about using his x-ray device to search for gold beneath downtown L.A., then he vanishes without a trace. I'm still not sure if he was the victim or the perpetrator of a hoax."

Edwards considered briefly, then rose. "Thank you for your time, Sam. Selena will validate your parking at the front desk."

Sam gave me a puzzled look as he got his feet. I didn't want to touch Edwards again, and was relieved when he didn't offer his hand. For an instant I thought Sam wasn't going to leave, then he turned away, his jerky movements conveying anger.

Once we reached the elevator and the doors had shut, Sam growled, "Well, that was a spectacular waste of time. What, we couldn't have had that conversation on the phone?"

Out of the heat now, in the air-conditioned confines of the elevator, I shivered. "I don't think conversation was the point of that meeting."

Sam turned to me, perplexed. "Then what was?"

"Well, I...I'd swear it was like he was trying to warn you."

"Warn me? About what?"

I shrugged, and Sam let it go.

We reached the car in the bowels of the parking garage, and Sam drove us up the ascending ramps. Rounding one corner, I saw a single space set off from all the others, with a large sign reading RESERVED FOR DON EDWARDS at the end. As the car turned past, Edwards appeared from a nearby elevator, but walked around his Ferrari and slid a cardkey into a lock beside a nondescript door. The door opened and he stepped through. Just then Sam rounded another curve, and the whole thing was lost from sight.

What the hell...where could that door possibly go? I almost voiced my question, but Sam was already irritated, and as long as he was behind the wheel he didn't need more aggravation.

Movie biz bullshit, I tried to tell myself.

But it felt like something more.

Chapter 3

"In their breeding habits, the lizards resemble the snakes…"
— *Eighth Annual Report of the New York Zoological Society* (1907)

God, I hated university parties. But they were a fact of life, like graduate school, and jobs, and lovers who leave.

The one that night, a week after the useless meeting with Edwards, was no different. I stood by the bar in a dark club, sipping someone else's expensive liquor and trying not to stare at the peeling skin on the neck of the wealthy doctor in front of me.

"So tell me more about folklore," he said, and I knew he couldn't have been less interested. If his pop-eyed gaze was any indication, the only subject he cared about was my cleavage.

I risked a side glance, hoping to find a tactful way around him. The free shots of añejo tequila were a luxury, the company was not.

The purpose of the party was to lull more wealthy alumni into donating to their alma mater. I'd received an e-mail from the university president, Bill Cressin, asking me to "represent the department," and God, I'd been naïve enough to buy it… until I'd arrived, decked out in silk blouse and the green skirt that Maggie had always liked, and my dean had instructed me to "do whatever it takes to get their financial support."

"Well," I said, trying to use another sip of the Patron to work up a smile, "it's a broad subject. What would you like to know?"

"Give me something local. Something—" and he actually winked at me here, "— sexy."

My skin literally crawled. In a far corner I caught a glimpse of Amanda Houston, another teacher in the Folklore Department, but she was laughing, apparently enjoying her conversation with a man whose back was to me. I looked past her and around at the display of middle-aged money—men with their perfectly groomed trophy wives, a few of the prettier young university staff or teachers who'd published something that'd made its way onto local bookshelves, Cressin throwing me a threatening glance—and I saw their skin glinting in the bar's heat, and blurted out, "Do you know about The Lizard People?"

The doctor (I'd already forgotten his name—Mankin? Kamin?) froze with a glass halfway to his lips, and his nostrils flared for a moment…then he chuckled. "Lizard people, eh? I think I may know a few of those already."

I stared at the shreds of white, scaly flesh hanging from his jaw, and hoped he wasn't a dermatologist. "Don't we all," I said.

The heat was making me perspire, and I tried to be discrete as I raised a hand to my face. First, the studio asshole, now this bar—what WAS it with these bastards?

The good doctor offered me an undisguised leer, and said, "Your red hair is lovely. If you'd like to leave this bunch behind, we could…"

Oh God.

I abruptly wished I were somewhere, *anywhere* else but in this bar, at this party, with these would-be angels who made me feel like something lower on the evolutionary scale. I thought back to another party, a year ago, when I'd been rescued…by Maggie.

Fuck, I wished she was there, right then.

Maggie would have said something that made me choke on the tequila and the doctor feel charmed. She would have led him on, practically had him writing a check before she'd grab me and we'd run out.

Like a year ago…

I had been living in one of the dorms with a roommate named Kimberly who I barely knew. In the evenings I usually wandered down to the common room, where a large TV would be tuned to a rerun of *Star Trek: The Next Generation*, among an appreciative audience I felt at home with. I wasn't exactly a Trekkie—I mean, I didn't wear pointed ears or read Kirk/Spock porn online—but I could recite along with a lot of episodes.

It was a Friday night, and apparently some sort of campus sports event had just finished (Football? Basketball? If it was sports, I wasn't interested). Suddenly the common room was flooded with noisy jocks, some openly disregarding dorm rules as they waved half-empty bottles of beer.

Oh great: Steve Crowe. He was classic good-looking California boy—blonde, tall, white teeth, solid build—and he'd been pursuing me for the last month. He was a business major, popular, and I found him completely dull.

"Hey, there she is," he bellowed as he spotted me and stumbled in my direction, while three of his buddies hooted behind him.

"Hi, Steve," I responded, with as little enthusiasm as possible.

He plopped his muscled bulk down onto the couch beside me, causing a small film major to frown and scoot to the right. "So, gorgeous," and I'm sure I flinched from his boozy breath, "when we going out?"

I'd obviously been too nice to him so far; I'd politely demurred, put him off. But tonight, I was irritated—*fucking* irritated. I couldn't enjoy *Star Trek* anymore, and I hated the way he tried to reach for my hair. I stood up and answered, "We aren't."

I turned to go—and felt his fingers clamp around my wrist. The shock that flooded through me was so fast and strong it was as if I'd been zapped with electricity, 50,000 volts of panic and fury now racing through my veins.

"Hey, c'mon, be nice," and the way Steve growled the last word was anything but.

I yanked my hand, but he wasn't yielding. "Let go."

He laughed at me. So did his friends.

"I'm not kidding, Steve."

"Say we're going out, and I'll consider it."

Fucker.

He grinned at me, a bigger animal with helpless prey; and goddamn it, I was weak and trapped, and I hated it, and I hated him. Fucker wouldn't release me until I agreed.

A silent moment was shattered when another woman appeared, seemingly out of nowhere, shoving Steve in the chest and saying, "Lay off my girlfriend, okay?"

In his shock, Steve's fingers sprang open; and before I could do anything I was being dragged off. Happily. Gratefully.

"Come on."

My savior was a stunningly pretty Asian woman, an inch shorter than me, with silken black hair and flawless skin. I'd seen her around the dorms before and admired her beauty from afar, but we'd never really met.

I let myself be led to the elevators; as the doors closed on us, she asked, "What floor?"

I punched the button, then fell back against the metal wall as the car rose. "Jesus. Thanks for that."

"No problem. I hate those fucking jocks. Think they can get away with any shit they want. Entitled pricks."

Her name was Maggie. She was a film major. Wanted to direct. Was happy to join me for a glass of red wine in my room.

And had propositioned me within twenty minutes.

I told her it'd been six months since I'd broken up with Charles, my last boyfriend, and weeks since my last date (with Jim). And I admitted to a few girl-girl fumblings in high school, but no other experience with women.

We were in bed together before the night was over, and the next day left me dazed, overwhelmed by wonder at what had happened…and newfound lust. There wasn't a minute that went by for the next week when I didn't think of her, getting turned on again at thoughts of her lips, her skin, her hands. A month later, we left the dorm and rented a one-bedroom place together. I'd never been with anyone who I wanted so much, and so often. We kissed in classrooms, fondled under trees at night, laughed at passersby who might have heard us in a study room at the library. I was so smitten that I never even thought about our future together.

That was my fatal mistake.

Maggie liked to party. I'm not talking about what we did

together, just the two of us, although that'd been the best party imaginable. No, I'm talking about nightly club hops, with drinking and white powders and a lot of other women, and I'd gone along for a while, enjoying the big bad coming out thing; but when I got my first stern lecture from a teacher, I told Maggie we had to cut back. Maggie, however, claimed she was making more connections through parties than school; so I finally let her go alone. Soon Maggie was talking a lot about Deena, a rising film exec who'd promised her a job.

Then, two weeks ago, Maggie had left me for Deena.

And now there was no one to rescue me from this party, from these old men who ogled me as I boiled in their heat.

I tried to say something, but the tequila and the temperature combined to make my head whirl. I had to clutch the bar for support.

"All right?" The doctor (*Kaplan. Of course, that was it*) put a hand on my arm, and I had to fight an urge to jerk away.

"Sorry. Guess I'm not used to good liquor." I set the empty shot glass aside. I glanced around for Amanda Houston, but she'd vanished.

Doctor Kaplan grinned, moved his face closer, and for a second I swore I'd seen, not canines, but fangs—long, yellowish, gleaming with secretions. "You should let me help. I am a doctor, you know."

Now the tequila—or was it his presence, too near?—was making me nauseous as well, and I started to sidle past him, to the right. "I'd like that, really, but…"

"What?" He moved to cut off any escape.

What the fuck was I doing? At that point I'd just about decided to tell Mr. Dean and Mr. University President to kiss my ass as it vanished out the door…if I could just get by the good doctor; except I really *was* drunk, and it was hard to find the way out, and—

"Ah, Miss Morgan, there you are."

The familiar voice cut through my confusion, and there was Sam West, putting a shoulder between the doctor and me. He'd even used "Miss Morgan," our private inside joke, a reference to legendary local architect Julia Morgan, and I was relieved he hadn't used my real name around Kaplan.

Pretending to suddenly notice the doctor, Sam smiled at the smaller man, even as he motioned me to the exit. "Oh, sorry, hope I wasn't interrupting something. But my TA seems to have forgotten that we had a late study project tonight."

If Kaplan responded, I never heard it—I was already away from him, threading my way through the rest of them, feeling their eyes on me, more than a little desperate to reach the way out.

A minute later we stood on an empty sidewalk, breathing in cool night air, and I felt a partial return of sobriety. Sam was beside me, looking down with genuine concern, not the thinly veiled sexual curiosity of the wealthy old boys in the club.

"Feeling better?"

I nodded, then uttered a small, bitter laugh. "I don't know what happened in there. Maybe it was the alcohol, but I don't usually have a problem with it, not like that…"

"Or maybe it was the *other* people drinking. I've never liked these parties, having to kiss the collective ass of L.A.'s elite just to try to keep my salary going for another year."

"You're telling me it never gets better?"

It was Sam's turn to laugh, then he pointed across the street to his car. "Let me give you a ride a home."

Normally I would have turned him down—it wasn't that far, and I didn't mind the walk—but tonight I welcomed the comfort and the company.

Tonight, Los Angeles was a city of predators; and I felt too much like meat.

Chapter 4

"...Shufelt['s]...radio x-ray had led him hither and yon, over an area extending from the Public Library on West Fifth Street to the Southwest Museum...All records were kept on gold tablets, four feet long and fourteen inches wide...Shufelt stated he has taken 'X-ray pictures' of thirty-seven such tablets..."
— *Los Angeles Times*, January 29, 1934

That night, after the party, I had the first dream:

I was in an elevator with Doctor Kaplan, but he didn't see me. The elevator moved silently upward. The doors opened, and we were in the reception area for Don Edwards' office. His secretary, Selena, sat behind the desk, and as Kaplan passed she looked up with a frozen smile, but no other greeting. I followed Kaplan—who was obviously a frequent visitor here—into Edwards' office, just in time to see the studio executive press himself up to the glass wall...

…then step through. For a second he was visible outside, suspended impossibly, then he vanished. He didn't fall; he simply winked out of being.

Kaplan was walking to the glass, not slowing his stride as he neared it…and I woke up, alcohol-sick and missing Maggie.

I was feeling physically human again by that afternoon, but somehow I couldn't quite shake off the effects of the dream. It was a Saturday and I had the afternoon free, so I did something that I could always count on to provide comfort: I went to the downtown public library.

I've always loved language, words, knowledge; I collect books and even keep a record of my favorite quotes (some of which I've used here). L.A.'s main library on 5th Avenue is like a church for me; the third largest public library in the U.S., it's a testament to the fact that not all Californians are only interested in the sun and surf. I often went there for the sheer pleasure of it: the stacks, surrounding me with imprisoned knowledge and lore; the glowing screens of computers and microfiche readers; the quietude and calm. Even the librarians seem possessed of preternatural gifts, as if they were somehow connected directly to the books, and so granted serenity.

I rode the escalator all the way down to the bottom floor, then turned left, leaving the sunny atrium behind to enter the History Department. I knew chances were slim of finding something about Shufelt or his lizard people that Sam had missed, but the library's website had once featured a section on urban legends, with mention of the lizard people, and I was hoping that a few of the staff might even have their own stories to tell about Shufelt.

Moving to an aisle I'd visited several times before, I pulled down a few books on local history and took them to a study table. A few moments of perusal left me making mental notes about a few other subjects, but no richer on the subject of Shufelt. I did text myself a note about a line I found in one of the books, regarding a tunnel that supposedly connected Northern and Southern California, with the library as one terminus.

I walked over to the main department desk and flagged down a clerk. "I'm looking for any information on a man named G. Warren Shufelt—"

I stopped there, because the young man was already smiling. "You and a few other people. A lot of stuff on the internet these days."

"Yeah, I guess there is. I'm working on a book about local folklore…"

The boy—because he couldn't have been more than 19, maybe 20—eyed me for a moment, then nodded to himself. "You don't seem like the usual nut asking about him. Hang tight for a minute."

He picked up a phone, punched in a number, and spoke softly for a second; finally he hung up and turned to me. "Somebody will be here in just a minute."

Somebody…? But I thanked him and stepped back to wait.

Three minutes later, a woman strode through the department's doorway. She was tall, unbent by middle age, with upswept hair that seemed obsolete even for the classic depiction of a librarian. She wore a trim skirt and jacket, and glasses as anachronistic as her coif.

She conferred briefly with the young man behind the desk, who pointed at me, making me feel a bit like a bacterium under a microscope. I tried to smile as the woman turned my way. "I understand you're looking for information on the Shufelt case."

"Yes. I'm working with a local writer—do you know Samuel West?"

"He wrote that book on Mexican folklore, didn't he?"

"That's right. He's working on a new one now, about local urban legends. I'm his assistant."

The woman peered at me, and for an uncomfortable instant I had the sensation of once again being six years old and under the scrutiny of Miss Graves, my stern first grade teacher. Then the woman's posture changed, and I knew I'd somehow been accepted.

"Perhaps I can help you with something. This way."

I followed her to a far wall of the department, where a card-key unlocked an unmarked door. As the woman motioned me through, she said, "Is your interest actually more in Shufelt, or the Hopi legends?"

"Why do you ask?"

She spoke over one shoulder as we traversed a narrow hallway with a few storerooms off to the sides. "You said Mr. West's book was on urban legends, but Shufelt was quite real…"

"Of course. Well, Shufelt and the lizard people are kind of all wrapped up together, aren't they?"

There was no response. Instead, we reached the end of the corridor and stepped through another locked door. The librarian had to flip on a light switch, and I was surprised to find we stood at the top of a rusting staircase leading down. I'd thought we were already on the lowest level of the library.

The short flight down finished at an old wooden door that the librarian opened. As ancient overhead bulbs flickered on, I saw long stacks leading off into the gloom.

"I thought the special collections were on one of the upper floors…"

"They are now. We don't really use this area much, not since the 1986 fire. If you can believe it, we once found a homeless man living in here."

She didn't bother to elaborate, but stepped past me, and not waiting to make sure I was following, vanished around the end of a row. I had to hurry to keep up, although I really wanted to stop and examine the books we passed. They weren't exactly dusty—this room was probably still sealed and climate controlled—but they all seemed to possess a patina of age. There were flaking leather bindings that were at least a century old, and ribbed vellum spines that I knew may have dated back to the 17th century. I wondered if the homeless man had gotten lost here, locked in beneath the surface of downtown Los Angeles, imprisoned with books that were impossibly old and held knowledge considered too obsolete or outré to be placed on public display. I halfway expected to spot a filthy face staring at me from between two aging leather spines.

I turned a corner—and the librarian was gone. I stopped, turned, looked around; I could still hear the woman's footsteps, but couldn't tell exactly where the sound was coming from. Where had I lost her? Then the sound of the footsteps stopped, and I realized I really did not want to be down here, alone… and why had we come here, anyway? What could possibly be down here that I needed to see?

"Coming…?"

The woman's head suddenly appeared around the edge of some shelves, then ducked away again. I walked to the end of the row, turned right, and found her standing before a stack of ancient cabinets…

…and a door, a door that made me stop and stare in astonishment: it was obviously very old, solid wood, set into a brick archway—a perfect companion, in other words, to the one Sam and I had found in the Chinese tunnel on the other side of downtown, except there were no gilt characters inscribed around the border.

"This door…"

"I'm sorry…?"

I realized the librarian was actually several feet to my left, digging through one of the old cabinets. I had assumed she'd brought me here to see this door, but now I realized that wasn't it at all. She glanced at the door, disinterested, then returned to the contents of the drawer she was rifling through.

"Oh, that? Just a utility hallway."

I didn't believe her. The same archway, the same ring in the heavy wood, the stories about secret passages beneath the downtown library…so I reach out and pulled. The door swung open, and I peered into a short, unlit access corridor lined with pipes and ducts.

I was both disappointed and relieved.

The librarian uttered an exclamation and removed something from the cabinet. She examined it briefly, then held it out to me.

It was an 8" x 10" glossy black-and-white photograph, obviously old, just starting to turn brown, but still in good condition. It was a clear portrait of a smiling middle-aged man, holding up some sort of contraption on tripod legs with a pendulum swinging from the center.

"That's the best photo we have of Shufelt."

Shufelt? This was him? He looked to be in his late 30s, with unremarkable features. No distinguishing scar, no fearsome squint to the eyes…the only unusual aspect of the entire photo was the device he held.

"Is that thing he's holding…?"

"The x-ray device that he claimed to have found the gold with."

I'd seen another photo from this same session in a reproduction of a 1933 newspaper article, but it hadn't been as clear as this shot.

"Do you think it would be possible to get a copy of this to use in the book?"

She pursed her lips, considering. "It's part of the library's permanent collection, but yes—we can copy it for you, and you should be able to use it."

"That would be fantastic. Thanks."

As the librarian closed up the cabinet, I looked at the door a final time, then asked, "Do you think…do you think the lizard people were supposed to be people who worshiped lizards, or lizards that had taken the shape of people?"

Eyes wide behind her black-rimmed glasses, the other woman gaped for a second, then barked a single ugly laugh and closed the door. "I think our Mr. Shufelt was either quite deluded or extremely gullible. Surely you'd agree, wouldn't you?"

I gave her a half-nod, half-shrug…

…even as I felt sweat drip down my side, and realized for the first time how hot the fucking room was.

Chapter 5

Pālīsa pāhūna vintsū nāngī ṭākato — On seeing a lizard
a scorpion puts down his sting.
—A Marathi Proverb

The photo of Shufelt arrived a few days later, and I was
Sam's hero(ine). He couldn't imagine how it had never turned
up anywhere before; I told him I'd used youthful wiles on a
middle-aged librarian. I think he believed that.

One night mid-week, we'd stayed late in Sam's office, grad-
ing tests. Sam had long ago tried to send me home ("you don't
deserve to put in these hours on a TA's wages") but I'd been
happy to stay and help him. I wasn't keen on the idea of being
home alone, torn between a paper I should have been writing
and a bottle of wine.

It was late—after eleven, I think—and we were close to
finishing up, when Sam realized he'd left his keys in the class-

room where he'd taught that afternoon. The room was at the other end of the hall from his office, and I volunteered to go retrieve the keys. Sam, preoccupied with the last few tests, was happy to let me.

The building was quiet as I headed down the corridor; it was strange to be there without the thrum of students. Even the air conditioning units seemed to be shut down, and I heard almost nothing beyond the sound of my shoes clicking on the linoleum.

I reached the classroom, opened the door, and reached for the light switch. For some reason the overheads didn't go on, but I remembered there was a small light on the lectern at the front. Sam thought he'd left the keys on a shelf inside the podium, so I shouldn't need the fluorescents to find them.

I made my way to the front of the room, the only illumination provided by outside light striped by the blinds, and a window inset in the main door. I found the small desk lamp, turned it on, and sure enough, Sam's keys were right where he'd said they'd be. I pocketed them and reached for the lamp.

"Miss Keffler…"

My heart shot into my throat, and I saw a shadow at the back of the room. How had I missed it coming in? And why did I know that voice?

"It's Dr. Maury Kaplan. We met at the alumni party."

"Oh. Yes."

What the hell was he doing here? He didn't teach at the university, and I didn't even know if he'd made a donation or not. I glanced at the door to the room and saw it had closed behind me, which meant he couldn't have come in since I'd been there. How long had he waited, in the dark…for me?

"May I call you Gillian? I was hoping we could talk a little."

I started to wonder if I could make it past him. He stood perhaps ten feet from the door, and I didn't think he could move very quickly…but I didn't know that for sure. Right now there was forty feet and rows of desks between us, and that gave me whatever infinitesimal measure of safety I felt.

"Of course, Doctor, but…wouldn't it be more comfortable in one of the offices—?"

I took one step toward the door—

—and he was somehow there between me and the way out, fifteen feet away now. I hadn't even seen him move. *My God, how could he do that?*

"Right here is fine."

Would Sam hear me if I screamed? Probably not, at the far end of the corridor with half-a-dozen classrooms and offices in between. And there was no one else here at this late hour.

"Alright, Doctor. What can I do for you?" My voice was shaky, but at least it hadn't broken.

He was still just a shape, a few striations of light limning his form, and I wondered if his skin was still peeling. He started walking forward, and I stifled the impulse to back away.

"That story you mentioned to me…about the lizard people…"

"Yes?"

He was still advancing. "What do you really think about it?"

"What do you mean?"

He was only a few feet away, coming into the tiny circle cast by the lectern light. His face was close enough to see the shreds of skin, looking gray in the slight illumination.

"I meant," he said, and was so near now that I could feel his breath on my cheek, "do you personally believe any part of that legend?"

I decided to answer honestly. "I think there was something to it. I'm still not sure what, but…I suppose it's not impossible that there was an early tribe in the area that venerated lizards."

He smiled at that. No, he *grinned*, an expression that was too big and made his teeth gleam yellow.

I did back away then, instinctively…and he followed. I was against the front wall of the classroom, feeling the cool chalkboard behind my back, my heart hammering, hating and fearing him.

The bastard actually sniffed me then, tilting his head up as his nose twitched; and he stared at me, hard. "You're really very pretty," he said. Then, after a small consideration, he added, "I'd like to keep you."

The notion of seeing red when furious had always struck me as a cliché — but later I realized that it was simply that I'd never been *that* angry before, not even with Maggie. Everything rational dropped away and I was suddenly on fire, and there was that scarlet film over the scene. "Doctor Kaplan — " I started to say, but he cut me off.

"You'd be well cared for — "

I'm not sure about all the things I said next, because they came from some nonthinking part of me, an animal brain reacting out of anger and terror. I have a vague memory of seeing him reach for me, and I told him that he had five seconds to back the fuck away before I started screaming, and I didn't know how he'd gotten into the room, but he could get out the same way NOW, and fuck his 'care,' and I couldn't just be used like that, and if I ever saw him again I would call the police so fast his ragged head would spin.

I don't remember if he said anything before he left, but at some point the red dropped away from my vision, the rage was gone, and I was alone in the dark classroom. My legs gave out, and I slumped to the floor by the blackboard, shivering for a while.

When I heard footsteps in the hall outside, I tightened even more, expecting him to return, to call my bluff…but then I heard Sam's voice, "Gillian…?"

"Sam—!"

I struggled to my feet, cold now, but not shaking quite so much, and the door opened and Sam was there, poking his head in curiously. "Are you okay? You've been gone awhile…"

"There was…there was someone in here…"

He paled and rushed toward me. "Are you okay? What happened?"

"No; I'm okay. He's gone. It was…it was Doctor Kaplan, from the alumni party."

Sam stopped near me, looking confused and worried. "Doctor Kaplan? Why was he here?"

"I think he's…well, stalking me. But he's gone now."

"Jesus." Sam's hands clenched into fists for a second, then he stared at my arm. "You're bleeding."

I looked, and saw three oozing welts on my bare upper arm.

Sam turned away. "I left my phone back in the office. We need to go call the police—"

"No, Sam." I wasn't sure I'd ever called him by his first name before, and it worked—he stopped to look at me. "Let's go back to your office, but we can't call the police. I'll tell you why there."

I had almost no idea what I was going to say.

Chapter 6

"…folk-lore is the record of the progress of a people."
—William Elsey Connelley (1899)

"It's not just folklore anymore." Sam had made a cup of tea for me, and found some gauze we taped over my arm ("that'll scar," he'd said, as he'd swabbed the cuts out) and when I thought over what I wanted to say, that was the first sentence that I came up with.

Sam frowned. "I'm sorry…?"

"This will sound crazy, but…something's been happening ever since we looked at the tunnel—the one by the Castle, that had once been part of Chinatown…"

He sipped his own tea, considering. Then said, "Go on."

"Kaplan's part of it, and…I think he's not quite…right."

Sam didn't respond; he just eyed me over the rim of his mug, his expression unreadable. Nervous, I went on. "He moved too fast, and his skin…but it's not just him. There are others, like Edwards, at the studio, and…and you think this is fucked up, don't you?"

"No, I don't. Because…I've had some strange experiences too."

My hand was shaking, and I had to set the cup down. "Like what?"

"A strange meeting with Bill Cressin yesterday."

Cressin — the university president. Wealthy, networked with the other elite, the one who'd told me to chat up the alumni at the party. "And?"

"He asked a lot of questions about my new book — specifically about the section on Shufelt and the lizard people story. And he knew things about the book he couldn't possibly have known — he knew about an introduction I've been working on."

We stared at each other for a few seconds, stunned and scared.

Finally, I said, "So what do we do now?"

"I don't know. They obviously have the upper hand, so…" He broke off, turning away, struggling with something.

"What?"

His voice sounded rough when he spoke. "I'm supposed to be the expert here, and I don't know what to do, or how to protect you."

"We're both in danger, Sam. I don't know why Kaplan just left, but I'm not sure I'd count on it happening again. They might be coming after both of us."

"I know, but…" he turned and looked at me, his expression fierce. "It's not me I'm worried about."

And from that look in his eyes, I knew how Sam really felt about me. It was all there, what I'd been too preoccupied to see, and what he was very good at hiding.

What I didn't know was how I felt about him.

"Can you take me home now?" was all I asked in the end.

When he dropped me off in front of my apartment, my "good night" was carefully impersonal.

Chapter 7

"Evolution is not a force but a process…"
— John, Viscount Morley (*On Compromise*)

Another dream that night:

Kaplan, Edwards, and Cressin were assembled in Edwards' office. They spoke together softly—too softly for me to make out anything beyond soft hisses—and at one point Cressin waved a hand towards the glass wall. For a second I thought I saw towers outside, unlike any I'd ever seen before. They seemed too sinuous, too glistening to be manmade…but they also seemed somehow unfinished.

The phone woke me.

I was panicked for a moment, and I snatched at the phone, still in the undefined terror of the dream.

It was Maggie. She knew my schedule, and knew I had an hour free for lunch today. She wanted to meet.

I agreed, then hung up, trying to make sense of both the dream and the call. Both felt equally real and unreal.

We met at a grill just across a street bordering campus on the south side. I arrived a few minutes late, and Maggie had already gotten a booth. She saw me and waved.

Whatever I'd expected to feel—hate, regret, rekindled desire—nothing could have surprised me more than what I *did* experience.

Nothing. I felt nothing at all.

I moved on wooden legs to the booth and sat across from her. It was busy with the lunch hour rush, and we both had to lean slightly forward to hear anything over the chatter around us.

"Hey, Gil. How are you?"

"I'm okay." I didn't ask her the question in return. Perhaps it was rude, but I truthfully didn't care.

A server saved me the trouble. Drink orders were taken, then the waitress vanished. I waited.

After a few seconds, Maggie began, "Listen, I'm really sorry. I know the way I left…it wasn't fair to you, but I thought it was the right thing, to make it—you know, a clean break."

I didn't answer.

She cleared her throat, and I knew Maggie well enough to know that she was nervous. "I just wanted you to know that…I felt bad about that. And I want us to still be friends. We can do that, right? Be friends?"

She reached across the table and laid her hand on mine.

I looked at her fingers—small and slim, with the nails she liked to keep long and painted crimson—and then I slowly withdrew my hand. I felt calm, strong, when I answered her. "I'm sorry, but we don't really have enough in common for that."

I pulled a five from my purse to cover the iced tea I'd ordered, then got up. She was staring at me, her eyes wide, as I said, "Oh, and Maggie—I really do wish you well with Deena."

I turned and walked out.

By the time I'd reached the street, I was caught up in a rush of joy so intense that I almost expected to lift off the asphalt. Seeing Maggie had made me realize two things:

That what I'd had with her had never really transcended sex. And that what I really wanted was a life with someone I could talk to, share with, exchange with, save and be saved by.

Sam.

His last class would be out in thirty minutes, and then he'd return to his office. I'd be there already, waiting, and I'd tell him.

"Miss Keffler…"

Someone had called my name, and because I was thinking of Sam I thought it was him. I turned, smiling—

It wasn't Sam.

The biggest man I'd ever seen stood between me and a black limo parked at the curb. He was easily seven feet tall, with broad shoulders that seemed ready to explode from the perfectly tailored business suit he wore. He was handsome, with cocoa-colored skin and short wavy hair, and he wore aviator sunglasses that hid his eyes.

I knew he was with them. If he wasn't one of them (and I didn't think he was—something about the way he carried himself said very human, ex-athlete) he worked with them, or for them. My happiness was instantly swallowed by dread.

"Yes?"

He walked closer to me and removed the glasses. His eyes were the dark color of his skin, his gaze impassive. "Miss Keffler…this is for you."

He held something out to me, and I took it. It was small, no bigger than my fist, but so heavy I almost dropped it. It gleamed in the sun, making me squint, the color…

Gold. It was gold, cast into a shape. I had to turn it to see:

A lizard head. Like the small jade I'd found in the tunnel, but this one from gold, and I had no doubt that it was solid gold throughout.

He was talking again, and I struggled to focus on the words. "My employer would like to use that to barter for an hour of your time. If you agree, I'll immediately take you to a location less than ten minutes away, where you won't be touched or harmed. At the end of the hour, I'll return you to wherever you like; and you have my employer's promise that you will never hear from him or his colleagues again."

I looked around the street, seeing pedestrians, shoppers, diners, drivers…a hundred pairs of eyes who might see me if I ran, shouted. But shouted what? He hadn't threatened me yet. I was in no danger—unless I got into that car.

"You said 'if you agree'…what if I don't?"

He looked away, then put the sunglasses on again before turning back to me. "In that case, you can expect the meeting to occur at some other time in the very near future, under less pleasant circumstances. And Mr. West would be involved, as well."

Ah, there it was—the threat. If I didn't go with him now, Sam was in danger.

"Can you at least tell me if your employer is Dr. Kaplan?"

Did I see a flicker of distaste cross his elegant features? "It isn't," he answered.

It was suicidal, of course, to go with him. Despite his poise, I didn't believe the part about me not being harmed, or only being gone for an hour. But I *did* believe that they could find me any time, anywhere, and that hurting Sam or I would be as easy as swatting a fly.

And then there was the heavy object in my hand. Forget that it was probably worth six figures; it was proof that the "employer" was one of them. If there was a chance I could emerge from this alive, knowing it was over…

"All right," I said, heading to the limo.

He was ahead of me, opening the door. As I settled into the luxurious interior, he pointed at a small cabinet before me. "Help yourself to a drink."

Not likely.

I was going to my death. I believed that, and I would do it sober.

Chapter 8

"Los Angeles is often called the City of Dreams, and the protagonists of some of its most interesting tales have vanished like those shreds of barely remembered dreams the morning after…"

— From Samuel West's *The Secret History of Los Angeles*
(work in progress)

He was right, at least, about the drive only taking a few minutes. He steered the huge car up into the Santa Monica hills to the north of the university. The houses got larger and were more hidden behind fences, the farther uphill we went. Finally he turned right and drove down a narrow street lined on either side with canyon wild growth; the street reached its end at a huge gate. He pulled up to a video camera, and after a few seconds the gate swung open.

The fact that my captor didn't care if I knew where he lived only confirmed my assumption that I was already dead. Acceptance had settled into me like a stone, tamping down everything else. At least I wasn't shaking.

The limo rolled along, past beautifully manicured grounds, to a gorgeous house that was a minor architectural masterpiece. It was stately, with touches of Regency style, but also featured long sweeping curves and a tiled roof. I'd briefly flirted with an Architecture major, and I wondered if I recognized the builder of this house.

The driver opened the door for me and motioned to the huge front entry, which stood partly open…but he stood by the driver's side of the car. When I hesitated, he nodded and said, "Up the stairs, then turn left when you're inside. I'll be waiting here when you're done."

Strange. He almost made me believe that this wouldn't be a fatal encounter.

I strode up the steps and entered through the open door. Rooms opened off a short entry hall. I turned to the one on the left, and found myself in a spacious sitting room…

…but a sitting room that was partly a zoo. Cages, tanks, and terrariums lined cabinets and shelves—at least 50, each with its own lighting system and tiny ecology. The enclosures all held reptiles of some kind.

Lizards, of course.

Lizards, in all imaginable sizes and colors. I saw iguanas, chameleons, horned lizards, and even the unremarkable local variety.

"Do you know the architect Paul R. Williams?"

I started and turned away from a lovely bright green gecko I'd been gazing at, and realized there was a man in the far corner of the room. He was an older man, perhaps late 60s, but with the kind of sheen bought by great wealth, which meant he could have been 80. He seemed harmless enough, dressed casually in a button-down blue shirt and slacks, and he was holding a white cardboard container in one hand.

"Williams designed this house for me," he continued. "I had him lay out this room as basically one big reptile cage."

"I thought I recognized some of the lines. Williams is my favorite architect."

"And mine. He was a remarkable man. Would you believe that he was once questioned by the police here, in front of a house he'd designed, because he was black?" He stood by one of the tanks, moved a lid slightly, and dropped something in. That was when I realized the pasteboard carton held live crickets. It was feeding time.

"I apologize for giving you cause for alarm, Miss Keffler, but I really did want to talk."

"And I guess the phones don't work up here."

He offered a small, wry smile. "I like to show off the house. Not many could appreciate it quite the way you and I can."

You and I? What kind of bond did this man think we had?

The more I peered at his face, the more there was something familiar about it; it wasn't an extraordinary face, by any means, neither handsome nor ugly. But something…I was sure I'd seen him somewhere before, maybe at the alumni party, or…

"Let me tell you why you're here. Oh, manners—can I get you something? Water? Coffee? Wine, or…?"

"Answers will do just fine."

"Good." Still holding the carton, he gestured to a chair; I could hear the crickets scuttling behind their white walls. "Please. Take a seat."

The chair he'd pointed to was made of curved, polished plywood. It looked familiar to me, and he must have noticed my hesitation. "That's an original Eames. Some called it the most famous chair of the 20th century."

What the hell; even if I survived this meeting, I'd probably never get to sit in a chair this expensive again. It was surprisingly comfortable.

He continued moving around the room, attending to his reptiles. "First off," he said, using his bare fingers to drop another squirming insect into a tank, "you should know: I'm quite human."

I believed him, although I wondered why it mattered to him to say that. I kept quiet.

"But you've had interactions recently with some who are not. At least one of them finds you most intriguing."

"Doctor Kaplan," I answered. Behind him, I saw a tongue shoot forth and ensnare a cricket, which instantly disappeared down a scaly throat.

My host nodded, and laughed slightly. "Not all of them approve of Kaplan's…hobbies."

"I certainly don't."

His laugh was bigger now, and once again I tried to match his face to a memory. "The doctor," he continued, after a second, "has essentially forgotten about you by now, but you should know: they're about to reach fruition on a project they've worked on for centuries, and they won't let anything get in the way of reaching that conclusion — not you, not Sam West or his book, *nothing*. So, what I wanted to do today really, was just offer you some advice: leave them alone, and tell Sam to do the same."

"So I probably shouldn't ask you who they really are, or what this project is."

"No. You probably shouldn't."

I thought it over for a moment, and then asked, "So why are you telling me this?"

He shrugged. "Because you interest them, you interest *me*. We have something in common, because they've held me in similar regard. In the past I helped them—I opened their tunnels, after they'd been sealed by cave-ins during the 19th century."

I looked at his bland features, wondering why on earth they would have found him so fascinating—

And I knew. Suddenly I knew where I'd seen his face, those ordinary features, the bland smile. But it was impossible: he'd be over 110 years old, and this man was probably 65…

Of course. He'd made a deal with them. In 1933, he'd discovered their tunnels and freed them, and they'd rewarded him with wealth and longevity.

"They gave you all this," I breathed out, staring around the house in awe.

He nodded and dropped another cricket. "Yes."

"Because you helped them."

There must have been more disgust in my tone than I'd intended, because he turned and looked at me, not even noticing a cricket that crawled over the lid of the carton. "They're not evil. You recognize that, surely."

I thought of Edwards and his callous disregard, Cressin and the way he saw me as little more than a whore for the university, and of course Kaplan. "No, I don't, surely." I pulled my sleeve and the gauze wrapping away to show him the three wounds on my arm. "From Kaplan."

For a moment he looked at the marks with interest, almost envy. Then he returned to the tanks, failing to notice the cricket that had now crawled onto his sleeve. "Ah. Well, I'm sure he didn't even know he'd done that. They're so far above us, it's easy to see how their motives might not be apparent."

"Above us?"

"Of course. They've continued to evolve while we've stagnated. They took on our appearance and integrated with our world only long enough to acquire the resources to complete their project."

He didn't notice the cricket as it leapt from his arm. It landed on a table, then a windowsill. I wanted to rush to the window and fling it wide, let the cricket find freedom, even if its life outside would be short and ultimately meaningless. But it jumped again and vanished out of sight behind a table, and all I could do was silently wish it well.

"How much of our world have they been running?" I asked.

He shrugged, then opened a cupboard door and placed the container inside. "As much as they needed to. But that's about to end: their project is almost finished, and when it is — they'll be gone."

"Gone?"

"Yes. To a…new home."

"And what about you?"

He gazed around the room for a moment, and his eyes looked moist. "I hate to leave all this, but…what they've promised to show me…"

Always the engineer — still pursuing conceptual gold.

"Are we done?" I asked.

He nodded. "I think we are. You'll remember what I've told you?"

"Yes."

He extended a hand. It was the same hand that'd held the crickets, and I was reluctant to take it, but I did at last. His flesh was dry but warm, and I wondered how long it would stay that way.

"Goodbye, Miss Keffler."

I asked the driver to return me to Sam's office on campus. As the car pulled up before the green lawn surrounding the building, I nearly bolted from the limo. I was a few feet from it when the driver called my name. I turned and saw him holding the fist-sized gold head out to me. I'd left it on the back seat.

"I think he really wanted you to have this," he said, seeing my reluctance to take it.

He waited while I thought it through. Were they buying me off? Did they own some part of me if I took this, just as they owned their pet human engineer?

Or did they already own me, regardless of whether I took their gold or not?

In the end, I stepped forward and accepted it from the driver, who smiled. "Remember: they won't notice you if you don't go after them."

"Do you know what they're doing?"

He didn't answer, but turned, walked to the huge car, got in and drove away.

And I went to find Sam.

His class had run late that day, and I had to wait outside his office for him. When he finally appeared, he smiled tentatively, until he saw my face.

"What's wrong?"

"Let's go in."

I waited for him to unlock the door and get settled, then I told him everything. About the meeting, the house, the warning. Lastly, I showed him the gold head.

"Oh my God," he said, feeling its weight, turning it over and over in his hands. "This is invaluable."

"I know, but…"

"So what are you going to do?"

I told him the warning had worked. I was scared, and I wasn't sure any of us would survive whatever this "project" was, and that they apparently didn't care if we went on or not. I told him I wanted to figure out some way to live whatever was left of my life.

He listened quietly. And didn't stop me when I left his office.

Chapter 9

"What works good is better than what looks good,
because what works good lasts."
——Ray Eames

I had the last dream that night:

I was underground, moving quickly, always downward,
through tunnels. Some of the walls bore the indentations of
tablets that had once covered their surface—gold tablets that
The Lizard People had recorded their history on. I knew that at
some point they'd used the gold for another purpose, and the
tunnels were empty now.

Finally I reached (or was shown—I truthfully didn't know)
a large central space. There was Kaplan, and Edwards, and Cressin, and dozens more like them. The walls of this chamber were
lined with things that might have been machines, or crystal-
line growths, or cocoons; whatever I was seeing, I knew it was

beyond my understanding. Suddenly an image appeared in the center of the room, and I'd seen it before, outside a penthouse office: it was some sort of city, made of architecture that no human Paul Williams or Charles Eames could ever have imagined. When I'd glimpsed it before, it hadn't been complete; but now it was. They began moving towards the image, simply vanishing as they did. I woke as the last one disappeared.

Even though it was early—so early the sun hadn't risen yet—I knew what I had to do. I got dressed, and nearly ran across campus.

Sam arrived forty minutes later.

"We need to talk," I told him.

"Of course," he said, leading the way to his office.

He sat, but I didn't; I was too keyed up. I told him first about the dream, and that I thought it'd been more than that.

He heard me out, and then after a few silent seconds, he said, "I had it, too."

We stared at each other, silent, afraid, and awed, then I dropped into the other chair. "So they've left, haven't they. They built themselves a new world, somewhere else, and they're gone, and we're still here."

He nodded. "Yes. We were never part of their plan. We served only to get them what they needed to go."

"Won't someone notice all these important people just vanishing?"

Sam thought for a moment, then said, "They didn't want to be noticed, so maybe they've covered their tracks, made sure there are reasons for their disappearance. Turnaround for the studio chief, retirement for the doctor, a lateral career move for the university president. Or maybe they can just make us all forget."

"Okay," I told him, "maybe. And we…"

He looked away. "We're like…insects to them. They swat at us, then forget us and move on."

I nodded. "Yes. Just…lower animals."

There was quiet, then I cleared my throat and said what I'd come here to say. "But I want my life to mean something to *me*, Sam. That's why I'm dropping out."

He flinched, almost as if he'd been hit. "What—? Why? You're so close now, why would you—?"

I cut him off. "We may mean nothing to them, but we can mean something…to each other. And that'll be hard if I'm still a student."

Sam started to protest, but his mouth clamped shut in surprise as I got out of my chair, walked around the desk, and took his hands. I pulled him up, and he let me. I embraced him, and after a few seconds he put his arms around me, and we felt like we mattered.

We stayed that way for a while, then I told him, "I'm a lousy cook, but a great shopper."

"I can live with that," he answered.

Chapter 10

"On the left are the disciples of sociology and biology, who prophesy that at some future stage in man's evolution all races — white, black, yellow, brown, and red — will be fused into a single, great, human race. On the right are the reactionaries who would damn a race today and through all of the tomorrows to come because it lived in savagery yesterday...The one looks to a remote future, the other to the dead past."

— Paul R. Williams (from *I Am a Negro*)

I did a dangerous thing a week later: I drove up to look at the house.

I wasn't too surprised to see that it looked strangely run-down, as if it hadn't been occupied for some time, and there were real estate signs around the property.

I left the university and found a job I loved at a bookstore. I moved in with Sam a few months later, and had never been happier. Sam continued to work on *The Secret History of Los Angeles*, but confined his chapter on the lizard people only to summarizing facts that others had already recorded. It worked; no one (or no-thing) came after us.

And I wrote this journal, because I don't want to forget. It remains my secret, just as the gold lizard head does.

One day I had to run an errand downtown, and I drove past the construction site, the one next to The Castle. It now held the framework of a tall parking garage, concrete pillars and iron skeleton rearing up out of what had been an open hole in the earth a few months back.

I decided to stop and say hello to Jim. He was working, and was glad to see me. He seemed genuinely happy when I told him about Sam and me, and said he wasn't surprised. I told him that made one of us.

I asked him if there'd been anymore news about the tunnel, and he stammered a little. He'd fought to save it, siding with Sam, but in the end commerce had won out over history.

"Probably just as well," I told him, not bothering to explain.

We said our goodbyes, and as I turned away, walking along a newly laid concrete pad, movement caught the corner of my eye. I looked and saw a small brown lizard, running along the concrete until it came to a drainage hole, where it vanished.

I wondered if it was the same one I'd seen months ago, in what now felt like an earlier life. I hoped it was. I hoped it had survived against the odds, and adapted to its new manmade environs, and was hoarding a clutch of eggs somewhere safely out of sight.

I hadn't known then how much we had in common, that lizard and I.

I got in my car and drove home to Sam.

MONSTERS
of L.A.

THE
ZOMBIE

THE ZOMBIE

The former gardener lumbered alone down the middle of
Wilshire Boulevard. Of course there'd been no traffic for
months, but some dim part of the gardener's mind wondered
about the lack of any movement whatsoever. Except for the occasional roaming squads of those hunting his kind, he seemed
to be completely alone.

It was hot today—August in L.A., after all—but he felt
nothing as he made his way west; his body was no longer entirely human, and he neither sweated nor panted. *They* controlled all his autonomic functions.

He had neither purpose nor goal. He sought only to spread
what he carried within him.

He passed the intersection of Wilshire and Santa Monica.
On his right, a once-famous fountain stood dry and silent.
Had he still needed water (and had awareness to realize that)
he might have rued the fountain's death. As it was, he simply
trudged on.

A few blocks farther on, he heard music.

It was coming from nearby—not from the trash-strewn
shopping area on his left, but the residential streets on the right.

He stepped around a wrecked limo sprawled across three lanes of traffic, and saw that there was some sort of barricade covering the entrance to the next street. The music came from there.

He walked toward it and saw a recently erected wall of solid brick and metal stretching across the length of the street, connecting to fences surrounding the end houses. The wall stood about seven feet tall, and had one barred gate set into the middle.

He didn't see the motion detectors he set off, but he heard the alarms. The music shut off.

The gardener froze at the sound of running feet. He knew the other, shrill noise meant danger, but he was held in place by the approach of living feet and voices.

He wanted—he *needed*—to get to them.

A young man's head appeared over the top of the wall, and he whistled loudly as he spotted the gardener. "Yeah, we got one out here. Looks like a pretty good one—not too far gone. We can use it."

Another voice answered, "Okay, I'll get a bag ready."

The gardener waited. He moaned once, wanting.

"You ready?" called one of those on the other side.

"Let's do it."

The boy popped up into view again above the wall, several yards to the side. "Hey, over here…that's right, douchebag, this way; I've got what you want, come on…"

The gardener moved to follow—and missed the door popping open behind him, two other teens emerging with a large canvas sack that they expertly dropped down over him. He struggled briefly, then the sack was firmly tied around his midsection, encasing him; and he stopped.

"That shut him down easy," one of the boys noted.

"Let's get him inside," said another. "Makes me nervous to be out here for long."

"Pussy."

The gardener let himself be pushed along; *they* had lowered most of his vital processes while breathing was difficult and sight impossible.

"What's Dulac got planned for this one?" one of the boys asked.

"That new thing with the treadmill and the batteries."

"Jesus. That's never gonna work. I almost feel sorry for this asshole."

"Don't let Darren hear you say that, or you'll be the one on the treadmill instead of Mr. Manobot here."

The boys led the gardener for a few moments, down the street, through a gate, the surface under his feet changing from asphalt, to grass, to stone. Finally he was brought to a halt.

"Mr. Dulac—got a good one here for ya."

He heard an adult voice. "Good job, boys. Get him fitted up, and let's put him to work."

After a few seconds the bag was removed, but before the gardener could react, a heavy gag was tied over his mouth. "No biting for you, amigo."

He was in a huge backyard that had been partially converted into a vegetable garden on one side and a work area on the other. He was led past a crystal clear pool, and rows of tomatoes and bell peppers (his eyes lingered on them, attracted without understanding why) to a treadmill that was hooked up to wires and transformers and batteries. He tried to turn his head, to shake the gag lose or chew through it, but it wouldn't move. He wouldn't be able to bite them, and that was his reason for being.

"Look at him jerking his head—dickwad is still trying to get to us."

One of his captors, a young man wearing a polo shirt and khakis, pushed him violently, and he stumbled onto a treadmill. His hands were wrestled into place near the rails on each side of the machine, and were handcuffed there. He stood dumbly, until the boy in the polo shirt got on the machine behind him and started walking.

"Walk, ya fucker."

The gardener stumbled and went down, and the metal restraints tore into his wrists. Blood flew and hit the ground nearby.

A boy in a sports jersey and baggy jeans leapt back in alarm. "Aw Jesus, Chuck, that was stupid."

Chuck leapt off the treadmill, then gestured at the gardener. "Hey—he's walking now, right?"

The boy in the jersey knelt by the spatter of blood with a kitchen blowtorch, cooking it until only a tiny, cracked black stain remained. "Can't be too careful with this shit."

The gardener kept walking, his brain not grasping why he didn't seem to move. He didn't feel the pain in his wrists, partly because his pain receptors no longer functioned, and partly because his wrists had already been repaired.

Nearby, he saw others like him, engaged in various tasks. A quartet were chained to some sort of large lever, pushing in an endless circle. Some had been trained to do slightly more complex tasks: one painted a wall, another tilled soil.

The gardener moaned softly; he wanted that job, not this meaningless activity. He'd been good at *that* once.

"Hey, check out his wrists…already healed over."

The two boys who'd chained him to the treadmill examined his hands; Chuck whistled softly. "That never ceases to amaze me. No wonder they're so hard to kill."

"Yeah, and too bad we can't make that work for us. We haven't got a doctor. If we get sick, really sick…"

"Pussy."

The boys wandered off.

The gardener kept walking. He had no sense of the passage of time, although at some point the sun vanished and the night grew cold, but his body temperature was simply adjusted so he didn't notice.

In the large house behind him, he heard voices, glasses, music, laughter.

A girl appeared before him. She was maybe 16, wearing shorts and a T-shirt, drinking wine from a glass. She was already slightly drunk, her eyes unfocused as she looked up at him.

"So you're the one they brought in today. I think that makes you number 73…or is it 74? I forget. Anyway, of course we've had to put down 40 of them, so there's only about 30 left. I hate it when they have to kill one. The way they have to do it — putting on those suits, then carving the poor thing up and burning the pieces — it's terrible."

He looked at her…and a soft whimper bubbled in his throat. Her eyes widened in surprise.

"Hey, you almost…that was like you almost understood me. But you can't…right? You're as braindead as the rest… aren't you?"

He groaned again.

She gasped, then grinned. "Oh, *wow*. This is *so* cool. Okay, look — I promise not to tell Daddy, because he'd probably have the boys rip you up."

From inside the house, an older woman's voice called, "Danielle —?"

"Coming." Danielle whispered to the gardener, "That's my stupid mother. She was nuts even before everything fell apart, but I better go answer her or she'll come out here. I'll see you tomorrow."

The girl ran back to the house, and the gardener continued to walk.

Danielle came back the next night. And the next. And the next.

Usually she just sat cross-legged on the grass in front of him and talked. Sometimes she cried. Sometimes she asked him questions and pretended he'd responded, or decided that his incoherent noise was the answer she'd hoped for. But mostly she just talked.

She talked about how rich her family had been, and how her mother had been obsessed with her looks until she'd gone for some weird wrap treatment, and she'd come back from it changed—even colder, more distant. She talked about how quickly the world had fallen apart, after the nanotechnology disaster that had started at Cedar Sinai with a doctor's desperate attempt to resurrect his dead wife, and had spread out from that single event like a butterfly's death-altering history. She talked about how her father had used his money to barricade the neighborhood and seal them in, and how all the wealthy neighbors had been happy to go along with his plan, and how they'd decided to use infected victims as a labor force.

She thought her father was even crazier than her mother.

She asked the gardener what it felt like—living with tens of thousands of tiny nanobots in his body, constantly repairing him, shutting down unnecessary functions like memory and cognition, constantly looking for other humans to repair. She asked him how many others he'd infected, with a bite — a single drop of blood or saliva transferred into another body, a drop carrying hundreds of self-replicating nanobots. She told him that she couldn't watch when her dad told the others to destroy one of the infected; she knew they could only be killed by rendering so much damage that the nanobots couldn't repair them, but it still made her sick. She asked him if he remembered anything from before — where he'd been born (Mexico? El Salvador? America?) if he'd had a family, what he did.

Mostly he just stared and walked.

But occasionally, some part of him not yet altered by *them,* would tingle in recognition. When that happened, he made some sound deep in his throat, loud enough to escape the gag; and because of that she came back every night to talk to him.

She told him he was her best friend.

He kept walking.

Early one morning, before the others were up, as the sky just started to brighten, she came to him…with keys.

"I don't think you'd hurt me if I unlock you. I hate seeing you chained up like that."

He didn't respond.

Danielle bit her lip, then walked toward him tentatively. His eyes followed her, but his head didn't snap towards her, straining to bite.

She unlocked the right handcuff, pulled it away from his wrist, and then stepped back.

He almost lost his footing and immediately grabbed onto the railing.

Danielle stepped in front of him and said, "You'll have to stop walking."

He stared and kept walking.

"No," she said, loudly this time. "You *have* to stop. Just go slower, then slower, and you'll finally stop." She even mimicked moving her feet slowly.

He watched—and his feet followed hers. The pace of the treadmill declined, and finally ceased altogether.

Danielle smiled and moved to his left side. "See? I knew you were smart."

She unlocked the left cuff.

He lifted his hands away, flexing the fingers. He had no idea how long he'd held onto those railings, but there was a small pleasure in no longer having to.

He stepped cautiously forward. The treadmill started to roll under him again, but he adjusted his feet and stepped down onto the surrounding grass.

"You can take off your gag," she told him.

He did. He wrenched the heavy thing away and threw it aside.

Danielle extended her bare arm. "Now you can bite me."

The gardener stared at the offered flesh, but didn't move.

She wiggled her arm. "Please. Do it. I want to be with you. I can't stand these people any more. Bite me, and we'll leave here together, and I won't remember them."

"Danielle—!"

It was a man's voice, and Danielle and the gardener both turned to see her father, the former billionaire Darren Dulac, rushing into his yard with an automatic rifle in his arms. "Dan-

286

ielle, honey, get away from that thing—" He waved the sleek, black weapon to the right.

"No. Don't kill him, Daddy. Please."

A woman joined Dulac, a woman whose face somehow gleamed with unnatural youth, even while her expression was dead. "Danielle, listen to your father. Stay away from that thing."

Danielle thrust her arm again toward the gardener. "Look at him—he won't even bite me! You have to let him go."

The gardener looked at all of them, and in that moment—whether it was the nanorobots controlling him, or his own vestige of conscience—he saw the situation about to unfold, and knew he had one chance:

He turned and began to walk out of the yard.

"See, Daddy? He just wants to leave."

The gardener's back was turned to all of them, so he didn't see Danielle's mother rush forward and wrestle her daughter out of the way as Daddy shouldered the rifle and took aim.

The bullets tore into him, ripping parts of him out, tearing open his midsection, and carving away parts of his head. The nanorobots inside him worked frantically for a few seconds, then began to fail as his bloodstream leaked out into the beautifully landscaped backyard.

He never felt any of it.

But the nanos in his head ensured that his sense continued to function for a few extra seconds, so he was aware even as he fell, landing with a thud on his left side. One eye had been destroyed beyond repair, but the other still functioned, and he saw Danielle, her mouth opened in a silent scream, tear away from her mother's grasp and rush forward to him, kneel and lap at the blood on his face.

The last thing he saw was her blank expression.

MONSTERS
of L.A.

ABOUT
THE STORIES

Consider this the supplementary materials, a la extras, on a DVD. It's not at all necessary that you actually read any of this, but—just as hearing a director talk about the making of a film can increase your understanding of and appreciation for the movie—maybe some of these little essays will add to your enjoyment of the work.

A few words first about the book's title and overall concept: Contrary to what you might think, I love L.A. I'm a born-and-raised native, and, with the exception of a few years spent in San Diego and one childhood year in Northern California, I've lived around L.A. my whole life. I can't imagine living anywhere else. Sure, the property values suck, there's too much smog and traffic, and sometimes the always-looming overlord called The Movie Industry feels as if it's magically sucking IQ points from three-quarters of the population…but there's also the weather, the wonderful community of true artists here, and the best expression imaginable of America the Melting Pot. Within twenty minutes of this couch I'm now sitting on, I can find authentic Thai cuisine, a Mexican *panaderia* with killer pastries, a Chinese herb store with hundreds of different teas, or a kickass Japanese

Taken from just above the Hollywood Bowl, looking southeast along the 101 freeway towards downtown L.A.

toy store. If I feel like going out, I can attend folklore dances from a dozen different cultures, see the best modern art, hit a performance by a legendary musician in a small venue, or catch a flick in one of the last of the grand old movie palaces.

I've done all those things and a lot more. I've worked a variety of movie jobs, I've worked almost as many nonmovie jobs, and I've known people ranging from homeless vets to Academy Award winners. One of my goals with *Monsters of L.A.* was to give you a taste of what my life in this magical metropolis has been like. Since the stories preceding this supplement were fiction, what follows here are the nonfiction inspirations behind the tales. I hope you find some of these anecdotes as interesting to read as they were for me to live.

Frankenstein

There was a real man who inspired my pathetic patched-together vet, and his name was Dan. He was a local homeless fellow who would occasionally ask to use the bathroom of the bookstore where I was working. Dan was a dapper, bright little man who walked with a slight limp thanks to his time in 'Nam, but he made the most of it—he wore a tilted porkpie hat, a tweed sports jacket, and would sometimes twirl his cane in true Chaplin style. He always spoke with perfect articulation and little verbal flourishes. When he caught your gaze, he held on with a directness you couldn't help but like.

I started to enjoy his visits, and he came in more often, sometimes just to talk. He complained about the same neighborhood shopkeeper that the rest of us did, except his reasons were better: We could only bitch about the asshole's attitude and pettiness, but he had kicked the shit out of Dan's girlfriend one morning when he found her asleep in the alley behind his place. Dan had pushed him aside, trying to get his dazed girl out of the line of fire, and consequently the asshole had filed a restraining order against Dan. At first I thought Dan might have altered the truth a little—not about the kicking, but about only pushing the asshole, who showed up the next day with part of his face bandaged. Then I realized it didn't matter, because the one the cops had helped with a restraining order was the shopkeeper who liked to kick sleeping women (that same asshole eventually threatened me with a baseball bat, and you can guess whose side the cops came down on *that time*—suffice to say I still have the bat).

Later, Dan's girlfriend went to a county mental facility; and he wasn't allowed to see her. He'd come in late one night, just before closing, and talked about his elaborate plans for breaking her out. They involved borrowing a Harley and an after-visiting-hours window climb.

That was also about the first time he asked to borrow money. He asked for 99 cents. Not a dollar, but 99 cents. I gave it to him, not expecting it back. But there he was four hours later, counting out a dollar's worth of pennies, nickels and dimes he'd panhandled. I actually felt shame when I realized I hadn't expected it back. Dignity was all part of Dan's style. And he paid interest, too: he wrote a poem for me. After he'd counted out the change, he asked for a sheet of paper and a pencil. I gave it to him, and he wrote this poem right he stood there. Here it is:

There's a thousand things
that people see

So much to live
so many dreams

But those that think
they own it all

Find out their lives
are very small

So should you see me
on the street

It's destiny that we should meet

So in the future
just have a smile

Cause I've been here
the whole damn while...

Okay, so it's not Keats, but it was honest and real, and I felt amply repaid. He wrote me more after that, and I've still got some of them. Sometimes he'd bring a friend in, and they'd both write, a little contest.

Then a long time went by when I didn't see him, at least six months or so. It was December when one of his friends finally came by one night and told me Dan had shot himself. On August 12. His friend shook his head and stumbled out.

I thought a lot about Dan after that. I read his poems and wondered what he could've been in another life, another world, one that hadn't used him and then abandoned him.

This story, then, is in memory of Dan.

Dr. Jekyll and Mr. Hyde

I really did live in one of the UCLA dorms for a year, and during that time a number of rapes took place around the campus perimeter, meaning that we female students were perpetually being warned not to walk the campus alone at night.

The horrors presented in this story are nothing compared to what I encountered during my time in UCLA's Hedrick Hall. I'll take a murderous transgendered doctor over bathrooms smeared in limburger cheese any day.

The Phantom

Part of what this piece is about for me is not just the plight of the central character, but also the sorry state of the place where she's staying—a once-great club on the Sunset Strip.

I have an interest in architecture and historic buildings, which some might consider ironic since I live in a town that has very few structures older than a mere hundred years; but L.A. still has a wonderful history, reflected in some very colorful architecture. Certainly the fictitious "Loco's" in this story reflects some of the history of the Sunset Strip's legendary Whisky-a-Go-Go, which closed from 1982 to 1986; fortunately, unlike "Loco's," the Whisky's been going strong ever since.

The real inspiration for "Loco's," though, was neither a rock club, nor located anywhere near the Sunset Strip—it is, rather, an amazing building called "La Caña" ("The Barrel") which I used to work next to. Located on Vineland Avenue in North

La Caña in NoHo

Hollywood, La Caña started life in 1941 as "the Idle Hour Café"; the building really is shaped like a huge barrel, making it a prime example of what is now called "mimetic architecture" (I far prefer that term to the cruder "novelty architecture") or buildings that look like other objects. In the early 1970s the building was acquired by Jose and Dolores Fernandez, two former world-class flamenco dancers, and turned into a flamenco nightclub. I'm not sure when Jose passed on, but by the time I started working next door to La Caña, it was the early '90s, the restaurant had been closed for years, and Dolores lived alone in the upper part of the barrel.

Dolores was eccentric…to put it mildly. She'd been born to a circus family in the Midwest—her father had been the strongman. Although obviously advanced in years, she still had the high cheekbones of a great beauty; and in addition to being a highly regarded dancer, she'd also been a starlet under contract to MGM for six months in the 1940s, during which time she'd dated Orson Welles and flirted with Ernest Hemingway (or at least that's what she told me). Unfortunately, Dolores was not only eccentric, she was also incredibly stubborn and more than a little delusional—she continually labored under the belief that she would be reopening La Caña soon, and she refused to consider selling the building. While she lived there, the place was literally falling down around her—she came running into our store one morning, panicked because one of the huge old restaurant sinks had just crashed to the floor. When our owner went over to check, he came back more than a little freaked out, telling us that in his thirty-second trip inside he counted at least six rats.

We wavered back and forth all the time on whether to call Social Services on Dolores or not. She was still lucid enough to get by, and she still possessed a considerable amount of the former diva's vanity, so we never did. Our store moved from that location in 2006, and we lost track of Dolores.

Dolores passed away in 2010. She left no heirs and no will, so apparently the State now owns La Caña. There's at least one gentleman fighting to give La Caña historical monument status, but I can't see how that's ever going to work—I fear the building itself is simply too far gone, thanks to years of neglect. I hope I'm wrong.

The Hunchback

This story is really about a 15-year-old boy named Lawrence "Larry" King. You may remember Larry because it made big news when, on February 12, 2008, this California boy was shot twice in the head in front of his schoolmates for the crime of being gay. His killer, 14-year-old Brandon McInerney, allegedly used a .22 caliber revolver to murder Larry, because a few days earlier, Larry had asked Brandon to be his Valentine.

Larry's slaying was deeply disturbing to me for a number reasons, but one of them is probably not so immediately obvious: the incident occurred in a medium-sized town called Oxnard, about an hour west of L.A....close enough, in other words, that it can be considered part of the great SoCal metroplex.

This was not the California I thought I knew. Perhaps it sounds arrogant or absurdly idealistic to admit that I've always considered my state to be a bastion of tolerance. I've been surrounded by people of different colors, religions, and sexual preferences my whole life; I grew up being completely baffled (and I still am) by hate based on race, or what you worshipped, or who you wanted to kiss. I always assumed that bigotry, prejudice, and homophobia were things that happened *somewhere else*. Not here, not in L.A. where we had West Hollywood and Thaitown and Little Tokyo and Artesia's thriving Indian community.

Larry's killing was the first of two events to occur in 2008 that shattered that illusion; the second was the November passage by California's voters of Proposition 8, which banned gay marriage. It certainly doesn't help that Larry's death seemed to be the lead-in to the rash of gay bullying that shook the country in 2010; it was almost as if California not only had proven it could be as backwards and hateful as anyplace else, but was out to lead the way.

Since then, California has taken a few steps towards correcting its mistakes. Brandon McInerney will be tried as an adult with a hate-crime enhancement; and on August 4, 2010, in a magnificently written response, a judge named Vaughn R. Walker overturned Proposition 8. Of course Brandon McInerney has filed a plea of not guilty (the case has yet to go to trial) and the proponents of Prop 8 continue to appeal Walker's ruling…but I still prefer to think (in that absurdly idealistic way) that California is returning to sanity after a wobble.

I don't really know much about Larry King; he was barely 15 when he was shot, and I doubt if he'd found his real talents yet, since very few of us do that early. That's why my Jordi Moore is 16: old enough, in other words, to have discovered his gift and begun to explore it. I hope Larry had that chance; I hope he'd already begun to dazzle friends with his creations. Unfortunately I doubt it—Larry was living in a shelter at the time he was shot, since he claimed that his adoptive father had abused him. Larry's short life seems to have been fraught with more turmoil and hardship than any child should have to endure.

Jordi doesn't survive, either, but at least he has a chance to explore his potential. That's one of the things that makes fiction great—it may not alter the terrible wrong done to Larry King, but perhaps, in some infinitesimal way, it can help us to understand what happened to Larry, and how a 15-year-old boy named Brandon could be so filled with hate.

For Lawrence "Larry" Fobes King (January 13, 1993—February 13, 2008).

Dracula

No collection of stories based in L.A. would be complete without something about actors. They are every-frigging-where in this burg. The cute girl serving you at the restaurant? She's got a stack of head-shots in the kitchen. The handsome boy texting while he waits for his order at Starbucks? He's hoping for information on an audition. I have no idea how many come to L.A. every year (tens of thousands? Millions?) but almost as many are constantly leaving town, going back to their home in Illinois or Connecticut or Arizona. They came here because all their relatives always told them they were as good-looking as those actors on TV, but unfortunately they didn't realize that a whole lot of other good-looking kids were hearing the same thing. So they spend six months, maybe a year in L.A., then back at home they tell their friends about how they worked two days as an extra on a Michael Bay movie ("I think I'm the guy in the white shirt behind that car crash") about when they met Charlie Sheen (well, they didn't really meet him, but they're *sure* that was really him they saw in that liquor store) and then they talk about what a horrible place Los Angeles is, and they live the rest of their lives trying to deny how miserable they are being the assistant manager of a chain restaurant in Indianapolis.

Don't get me wrong—I actually love actors. In many ways, I think actors are close kin to writers—we're both in the business of building characters, after all, and we're both subject to constant rejection. I've had some wonderful, creative collaborations with talented actors, and heck—I live with an actor…but one who walked away from the biz *after* he'd achieved a measure of success, when he saw how the strange combination of competition and pampering often turned his peers into monsters. When I thought about what I'd do with Dracula, a character who is famed for his seductive glamour, his arrogance, and sucking the life out of those around him, the answer was obvious.

Originally my Dracula was going to be (like my Frankenstein) a human who utilized the legendary monster's attributes, but as I thought more of the story, the appeal of actually turning Dracula himself into a movie star was just too strong.

The Bride

This (unlike the world of Hollywood) is the only sequel in the collection, so there's really no more to be said about it here.

The Mummy

I detest the idea of spas and beauty treatments, and find it highly ironic that one of my doppelgangers (another Lisa Morton) is a professional reviewer of beauty products.

The Invisible Woman

I went through a strange period of about two years when I was surrounded by crimes or potential crimes that no one else seemed to care about. Three in particular stand out:

The first was a burglary that occurred at a bookstore I was managing. The thieves had broken in overnight, ransacked our safe, and left behind the heavy crowbar and hammer they'd used—complete with obvious fingerprints. I, of course, was certain this would lead to an easy arrest and conviction. Well, the cops took two days to show up, spent about five minutes taking my report, and turned to go. "Wait," I called after them, "aren't you taking these tools?!" No point, they told me. "Hey, they're good tools—you keep 'em." They were good tools—I've still got them. Of course I never heard any more about the burglary.

Second incident: In the early morning hours of June 4, 1988, my stepfather passed away very unexpectedly—two days before the beginning of principal photography on my first movie, *Meet the Hollowheads* (then titled *Life On the Edge*). He was 66 and in nearly perfect health; he'd had a physical not long before and had passed with flying colors. There was simply no reason for this robust, wonderful man to die in his sleep. At about 4:30 a.m., my mother awoke when she heard his head hit the top of the bed; by the time the paramedics arrived, he was dead. My mother was of course shocked beyond comprehension, and had no response when the hospital asked if she wanted an autopsy done. She and I have since commented on the fact that she could have murdered him and gotten away with it; I know the big cities (this was in Portland, Oregon) are overworked and routinely don't autopsy elderly people (and presumably can spot a homicide case quickly) but it did seem odd to us, since there was no obvious cause of death (his death certificate just listed a standard "cardiac arrest" thing…which frankly still seems unlikely to me).

Third incident: One night, about two blocks from where I live, I really did see what looked strangely like two guys loading a bagged body into the trunk of a car. They were so open about it that I'm sure it can't have been that…but the image has stayed with me for twenty years.

The confluence of these events (and a few other minor ones) made me realize that our crime television series and movies are all bullshit, and exist in part to lull us into believing that we're safe. We're not, and those of us who don't fit any suspicious profiles could probably get away with an insane amount of crime, if we wanted to. We're the invisible ones, in other words.

The Mad Scientist

This was actually one of the hardest stories for me to write, as evidenced by the fact that it's also the smallest; in fact, if we're completely honest, it's really not much more than a prologue to the zombie story. The reason: Southern California has always been a home to technology research, but the nature of the technology has changed so drastically during my lifetime that I'm no longer familiar with it. When I was a kid growing up in the San Gabriel Valley, tech equaled aerospace. The aerospace industry was a gigantic part of life in SoCal; heck, my dad was employed in it, working with the Air Force and

NASA designing flight suits and helmets for the Gemini and Mercury space programs (I wish I still had a fraction of the cool early space stuff Pop used to bring home to me!). Aside from the government projects, we also had the big companies like Rockwell and Lockheed here, and they employed an awful lot of people. Our aerospace industry was even dramatic, like when Christopher Boyce, working out of TRW, sold spy satellite secrets to the Russians and inspired the story of *The Falcon and the Snowman*.

But by the end of the 20th century, SoCal's aerospace companies had all but vanished, only to be replaced by new technological firms, mostly internet start-ups or medical research firms. Irvine, an hour south at the southern tip of Orange County, started to house a lot of these firms.

I'm sorry to say that I know virtually no one working in L.A.'s new high-tech industries. Once upon a time, if you lived here and weren't a hermit, it was practically a guarantee that you knew someone in the aerospace industry, but the same can't be said of these new tech firms. Hence, the idea of doing a mad scientist story set in 21st century Southern California left me at sea, and resulted in the short-short presented herein.

Oh, and I admit unashamedly that the name "Dr. West" is a tip of the hat to H. P. Lovecraft, Stuart Gordon, and Jeffrey Combs.

The Werewolf

This story had an unusual origin: it was birthed as a one-act play that became part of an evening of one-acts entitled "Spirits of the Season." This production, which ran from October 6, 1995 to November 19, 1995, also included plays about a ghost

Lonnie Schuyler as Monck, Erica Hade, and Darryl Armbruster as Hardy in the 1995 production of "Howlin' Monck and the Death of Music."

("Silver Nitrate Blues"), a vampire ("Too Young To"), and a zombie ("Falling to Pieces"), and was immensely successful. The werewolf play, under its original title "Howlin' Monck and the Death of Music," was possibly the stand-out of the evening—the *L.A. Times* said "*Grand Guignol takes center stage in the closer, 'Howlin' Monck and the Death of Music'…like the first piece, what could have been stupid horror tricks turns into a real drama with this committed cast,*" and the L.A. Weekly said that *"Monck" "score(d) a stake to the heart."* "Monck" was popular for years after in our theater company, and every young actor had to try the eponymous wolfman at least once.

When I sat down to think about what was really behind the werewolf legend, I immediately went to loss of control and gleeful excess. Strangely enough, that led to thoughts of rock stars, and Howlin' Monck was born. Since it was already set in California, it felt right at home in this collection.

The Haunted House

This is obviously another ode to my affection for L.A.'s architecture, but a more obvious one than "The Phantom."

Angelino Heights is a real place, located near Echo Park just northwest of downtown L.A., and it really is an amazing conglomeration of vintage houses. However, the Donegan house in this story is really based on another house that sadly no longer exists: A Bunker Hill landmark called The Castle. Ironically, I didn't know of the existence of The Castle—an immense Victorian mansion built probably in 1888—until after I'd written (and sold) my novel *The Castle of Los Angeles* (my "Castle" is actually based on another L.A. landmark, the collection of artists' lofts known as The Brewery). The Castle was an amazing construction that really did become a boarding house at one point, and really was reputed to be haunted by the ghost of a suicide. This glorious house came to its own tragic ending: After Bunker Hill was razed for redevelopment, The Castle was one of two buildings left and funds were acquired to move the house a short distance away to preserve it. Unfortunately, on October 6, 1969—just over six months after the relocation—The Castle and the other remaining structure, the Salt Box, fell victim to arsonists and burned to the ground.

Several of the names in this story are tips of the hat to The Castle, which was constructed by Reuben M. Baker and later owned by Daniel Donegan, who may have been the first to dub it "The Castle."

Angelino Heights, 2011.

The name I chose for my reality show (*Ghostmasters*) is also an in-joke: *Ghostmasters* is the name of a terrific book by Mark Walker about the magicians who once staged ghost shows and fake séances in movie theaters during (mainly) the 1940s and 1950s. As a strict nonbeliever in paranormal activity, I wanted to give my fictitious series a name that included a touch of irony.

Cat People

I love folklore and mythology, and I suspect that most people might be surprised to discover that Los Angeles has a rich and varied urban folklife, thanks in no small part to the mix of ethnicities and cultures here. Several other works by me, including "The Urban Legend" story herein, make use of my favorite local legend, that of the Serpent or Lizard People who supposedly once lived in tunnels lined with gold beneath the streets of L.A. (there was even supposed to be a secret opening to their tunnels in the basement of the downtown public library). Tied into the Serpent People's saga was the real story of one G. Warren Shufelt, an engineer who, in the 1930s, convinced the city of L.A. to give him permission to dig up parts of the city in search of that reptilian gold (he kindly offered to split it with the city).

However, one of my other favorite stories was that of "La Japonesa," a catwoman spirit said to roam the hills around El Monte in the San Gabriel Valley (one supposed eyewitness even posted online a manga-like sketch of her). All of the background given for this legend in my story is culled from real sources, especially the work of folklorist Alfred Avila (see his *Mexican Ghost Tales of the Southwest*). I love not just the imagery of an Asian female half-human cat spirit, but also the wonderful melting pot medley of Mexican, Japanese, and Southern Californian influences.

The Creature

La Brea Tar Pits.

I'm a lifelong fan of the La Brea Tar Pits. C'mon—a primordial swamp of bubbling black goo smacked down right in the middle of one of the world's most modern metropolises? How can you not love a 100% natural whole rotten-heart-of-the-city metaphor thing?

The Alien

As a kid growing up in the San Gabriel Valley (just to the east of downtown L.A., for those of you who aren't familiar with SoCal geography) my great-grandmother lived on Huntington Drive just around the corner from the Los Angeles County Arboretum, and I practically grew up there. I still adore the Arboretum, and try to visit at least once a year. It's a little different these days—mainly they charge admission

One of the Los Angeles County Arboretum's stranger specimens.

now (at the current price of eight bucks, it's still a great deal)—but in most respects it hasn't changed a bit. It still has the main wide area with the fountains when you first enter, the exotic plants are just to the north, the screaming peacocks roam free (although when I was little, they also wandered the streets of nearby San Marino), and the lake in the center of the park looks primeval. (So primeval, in fact, that for most of my life I labored under the bizarre notion that *Creature From the Black Lagoon* had been shot there, at least in part. It wasn't, although many other movies and television shows have been.)

Whether due to its size, the admission fee, or simply that most of the public has no interest in botany or history (the Arboretum also houses several historic buildings) the Arboretum seldom seems crowded, and it's easy to wander into some far corner and imagine you're quite alone there. That, and the truly strange appearance of some of their more exotic plant specimens, inspired this florid and floral tale.

Kaiju

People who don't live in California think that those of us who do must be Beach Boys devotees who live out our lives tanning by the seaside and chasing waves.

As a kid, I did like the beach (and the ocean—my dad's a fisherman and we always had boats) but—like so many other parts of Southern California—it's changed considerably over the years. I'm not anxious, frankly, to go anywhere near the waters of the Santa Monica bay, which has seen more than its fair

The author at 9 with a barracuda caught off the coast of Southern California.

311

share of sewage spills and other unnatural disasters; horror stories abound about everything from used hypodermic needles hidden in the sand, to boardwalk thieves. The beaches are now perpetually shoulder-to-shoulder, and of course, thirty years ago no one paid much attention to the notion of skin cancer. We were mainly concerned with getting one more of those sunburns that was so painful it gave you flu-like symptoms for the next two days (been there, done that—but I haven't died of skin cancer yet).

I haven't been to the beach in years, and that's fine. I'll leave it to the tourists and those willing to brave parking nightmares and toxic water.

Oh, and my favorite kaiju movie is *War of the Gargantuas*.

The Devil

This story was originally going to be something very different, but when I looked at the overall collection and how I wanted it to represent my Southern California, I saw one big gap: amusement parks.

Yep, we've got 'em and we love 'em. I suppose it's because our year-round temperate weather is easy on outdoor attractions; throw in access to both the film industry's artists and the tech firms' engineers, and we were practically destined to give birth to the modern amusement park in 1955, when Disneyland opened just a few minutes south of L.A. Since I was born not long thereafter and less than an hour away, and since my folks loved the park, we went there at least once a year (this was back when you could still get on rides in less than half-an-hour and didn't have to battle shoulder-to-shoulder for sidewalk space with hordes of obnoxious baby strollers). We also frequented Knott's Berry Farm when it was little more than a chicken restaurant with a mock-up of an old ghost town in the back lot (I've never forgiven Knott's for turning the quaint old tourist attraction into an expensive collection of roller coasters).

As a kid, I loved the Devil. Really, he may have been my favorite monster, partly because he could be wily and funny as well as scary, and partly because I loved the way he looked (I used to doodle devil portraits in school by the dozens). My favorite Halloween mask as a child was a cheap, bright red plastic devil mask, which I probably wore for at least two trick-or-treat expeditions (I still remember the smell inside that mask, a mix of plastic, sweat, and breath). Amusingly, there were delightful devils to be found at both Disneyland and Knott's: the former has "Mr. Toad's Wild Ride," which climaxes when your little car collides with a train and sends you straight to a Hell inhabited by dozens of little potbellied, twittering devils; and Knott's once had a 12-foot tall mock-up of an erupting volcano, complete with an inset window where you could watch a miniature devil crank the machinery that caused the eruptions (I *really* liked this hard-working imp, and wish I had taken a good photo of him before they consigned him to the trash heap of amusement park renovation).

If you think this story might also have something to do with my vast affection for Disneyland's "Haunted Mansion"… you'd be right.

The Slasher

This story is historically interesting for me because it was the first horror short story I ever wrote (not counting a few idle doodles in school). Up until that point (this would have been around 1990) I'd written nothing but screenplays and plays; I'd had modest success as a screenwriter, but had produced nothing I was particularly proud of (although I still have a nostalgic fondness for my first film, *Meet the Hollowheads*). I'd first moved into small theater, where I liked the control of being able to direct the material I'd written, and then—influenced largely by the short fiction of Dennis Etchison—I started writing short stories.

In the beginning, I had absolutely no idea what to do with the stories; I barely even knew proper manuscript format (I'd gotten that from looking at some Harlan Ellison manuscripts for sale in the local used bookstore, before I started working there). I wrote about a half-a-dozen of these tales, printed them out, and tossed them into a three-ring binder for God only knows what eventual purpose.

One evening my partner in theater, Rocky Heck, held a staged reading of a play by a local writer named Roberta Lannes. Roberta had been discovered by Dennis (in a UCLA writing class he taught) and he'd published her brilliant, horrifically cathartic short story "Goodbye, Dark Love"; Rocky had met her through Dennis, and found out she had a one-act play. Even though the reading didn't go that well, Roberta and I fell into each others' orbits like two long-lost sisters, and we've remained best friends ever since. About the second time we met, I think, I asked Roberta to look at my little notebook of stories. She did, and I was thrilled when she told me she thought they were all publishable (two of them— "Sane Reaction" and "Love Eats"—did indeed become two of my earliest sales).

This story, under its original title "Crack," was the first one. It was inspired by an actual visit to a weird system of ravines in the Santa Monica hills; a friend took me there one day, and we looked down from overhead at the collection of used furniture below and realized someone was living in there. We never could figure out where the opening was, and the idea of someone living in cast-off furnishings inside these crumbling runnels really disturbed me (sadly I can no longer remember the exact location of these ravines, and I wonder if they still exist).

I never did try to shop this story around. I think it's because, shortly after I wrote it, I developed an intense dislike of first-person stories in which the narrator couldn't possibly have survived. Despite my vast affection for Billy Wilder's *Sunset Boulevard*, these sorts of tales still make me crazy.

"Crack" is presented here with no real changes to the original text other than the title. It's interesting to me that even in the early '90s—when the economy was still comparatively rosy—I was already writing about protagonists who were impoverished and unemployed.

The Killer Clown

I wanted this story to combine two things I'm inordinately fond of: Halloween, and a famous store called Circus Liquor.

The reason I love Circus Liquor has nothing to do with drinking—I've never even been inside the place, frankly—but everything to do with their giant neon clown sign, which really *is* as creepy as the one I've tried to describe in the story. Search for "Circus Liquor" online, and you'll get photos, blog entries, YouTube videos, and Facebook groups all attesting to that giant clown's popularity. And yes, he really is located on Vineland (at the corner of Vineland and Burbank Boulevard in North Hollywood).

And of course I wanted a Halloween story in this collection. I'm (ahem) something of an expert on the holiday, having recently released the 2nd edition of *The Halloween Encyclopedia* (which included a new entry on clowns, by the way) and I have a life-long love of Halloween in Los Angeles. Some of my best memories of childhood center on trick-or-treating up and down 9th Street in Arcadia, and I'd originally considered a story about Jason and Freddie as kids trick-or-treating in the 'burbs, but opted instead (wisely, I think now) for this little venture into bizarro horror fiction, with a side helping of L.A.'s world-renowned West Hollywood Halloween celebration.

Oh, and there's a really silly in-joke buried in here: if you don't speak Spanish, look up the name of the wine they're searching for, in any online translator.

The Urban Legend

This novelette is actually a prequel to my (as yet unpublished) third novel, *Malediction*. Sam West is one of the protagonists of that book, which takes place about three years after the events of this tale (which I think of as "The Lower Animals"). Gil—who is Sam's wife in *Malediction*—ended up being a supporting character, but I liked her so much that I felt guilty about how the necessities of the novel's plot gave her short shrift. Hence, this novelette is my attempt to expunge that guilt. I hope Gil forgives me.

Virtually all of the folklore background given here (I've already spoken a little about this in my essay on the background behind the "Cat People" story) is real, and has fascinated me for years, especially the crazy notion that the basement of L.A.'s magnificent downtown public library has a secret doorway leading to The Lizard People's tunnels. The story about the homeless man living in a forgotten basement of the library is true, and was relayed to me by a friend who had worked at the library. Ironically enough, my friend had never heard about The Lizard People until I asked him about it; but shortly thereafter he said there were a lot of people asking about the legend and about Shufelt. Other parts of the history—like the 1871 riots that killed nearly 20 Chinese—are also sadly true.

However, The Castle is a big fat lie, and an obvious in-joke reference to my novel *The Castle of Los Angeles*.

Also, this tale represents the apex of my architectural obsession. Other than to note that I share Gil's affection for the work and life of Paul Williams, I'll shut up about that now.

The Zombie

I almost feel like I should apologize to my city for ending this collection with a story that paints L.A. in such a bad light. However...there was really no way for me to produce a series of stories exploring the meaning of Los Angeles without something about the economic disparity here. Obviously the gap between rich and poor has widened everywhere in the U.S., as the middle class has officially moved onto the endangered species list…but it's been particularly painful to watch happen in L.A. The city that practically invented the suburb almost doesn't have them any more, or at least doesn't have them like it used to. As housing prices in Southern California have skyrocketed, certain suburbs—like the one I grew up in—have come to resemble ghost towns. Houses that have been vacated by owners who could no longer afford to live in them sometimes sit for months or years, seemingly abandoned, while those houses that are still occupied look increasingly rundown, since their residents no longer have the money needed to keep them fixed up. We are the third largest Spanish-speaking city in the world, and yet the insane amounts that apartments rent for here mean immigrants often squeeze multiple families into one- or two-bedrooms residences, resulting in unsafe living conditions (and subjecting all of us apartment-dwellers to yearly city inspections, whether we want them or not). Meanwhile, those of us who grew up here buying into the great Angeleno dream—work hard and you'll be able to buy your own pastel colored house with a swimming pool and an orange tree in the backyard—watch two-bedroom, one-bath houses the size of our apartments go for nearly twenty times what we make in a year, and realize that we will likely die without ever experiencing the pride of home ownership.

All the while, we live side-by-side with the ostentatiously wealthy, who sit next to us on the streets in their freshly waxed new convertibles and occasionally toss us table scraps of work, underpaying us (and yes, I include myself as a screenwriter in this) because we are desperate. We console ourselves by watching the offspring of these billionaires flame out spectacularly in public, and imagine what we could do with the money they've just spent on one purse. Or perhaps we point at their wives, with skin stretched too tight from too much time spent in a plastic surgeon's office, and we pretend we're superior.

So why stay, when any of us could move across the country and buy a four-bedroom house with acreage and end up with mortgage payments less than our current monthly rent?

Well, forget that I have family, friends, a job, and roots here…L.A.'s a magical place. Take today, for example: As I write this it's early February and the rest of the country is groaning beneath the weight of more snowstorms, but here it was glorious, with blue skies and short sleeve temperatures. This week I'll probably have an amazing Thai noodle dish for lunch one day, and hit a great cheap Italian deli the next. I'll chat (in the flesh) with fellow writers and book lovers, maybe pick up a half-pound of oolong tea from my favorite Chinese herb store, and complain when I have to drive around yet another film crew creating dreams on a local street. Maybe I'll get really ambitious and finally embark on that hike through Griffith Park that takes you to Bee Rock, which supposedly resembles the profile of Petranilla de Feliz, the 19th century Californio who cursed Griffith Park.

Whatever it is I end up doing this week…I'll love it, because I'll be doing it in L.A., my hometown and my home.

(All photos were taken by the author or the author's relatives)

About the Author

LISA MORTON is a four-time Bram Stoker Award-winning author, a screenwriter with such cult favorites as *Meet the Hollowheads* to her credit, and a world-renowned Halloween expert. A native and lifelong resident of Southern California, her short stories have appeared in dozens of award-winning and acclaimed anthologies and magazines, including *Zombie Apocalypse!*, *Unspeakable Horror: From the Shadows of the Closet*, *Horror Library Volume 3*, *Dark Delicacies*, *Mondo Zombie*, *Dark Terrors 6*, *The Museum of Horrors*, and *Midnight Walk*. Her two previous books from Bad Moon were the critically praised novellas *The Lucid Dreaming* (winner of the Bram Stoker Award for Long Fiction) and *The Samhanach* (nominated for the Bram Stoker Award). *Monsters of L.A.* is her first collection.